No small victory

No small victory

CONNIE BRUMMEL CROOK

Fitzhenry & Whiteside

Published in the United States by Fitzhenry & Whiteside,
311 Washington Street, Brighton, Massachusetts 02135

www.fitzhenry.ca   godwit@fitzhenry.ca

10 9 8 7 6 5 4 3 2 1

Library and Archives Canada Cataloguing in Publication

Crook, Connie Brummel
          No small victory / Connie Brummel Crook.

For ages 8-12.

ISBN 978-1-55455-169-9
          I. Title.

PS8555.R6113N6 2010   jC813'.54   C2010-900232-6

U.S. Publisher Cataloging-in-Publication Data

Crook, Connie Brummel.
   No small victory / Connie Brummel Crook.
   [160] p. : cm.

ISBN: 978-1-55455-169-9 (pbk.)

1. Courage – Juvenile fiction. 2. Teenage boys – Juvenile fiction. I. Title.
[Fic] dc22   PZ7.C766Ns 2010

Fitzhenry & Whiteside acknowledges with thanks the Canada Council for the Arts, and the Ontario Arts Council for their support of our publishing program. We acknowledge the financial support of the Government of Canada through the Book Publishing Industry Development Program (BPIDP) for our publishing activities.

Cover and interior design by Erik Mohr
Cover image: iStockphoto.com/Imagine Golf (Farm), iStockphoto.com/VegaBlue (Girl)
Printed in Canada

With fondest memories to my friends,
Madeleine Davidson Kempt and Archie Davidson
and in memory of Muriel Humphries Bowman

Acknowledgements

My many thanks to the following:

My grandson, Ryan Floyd, for composing the poem to match the original chant, Here Come the Kids from Bug Town.

Eileen Balfour, of Peterborough, for expert advice from her own experience in raising chicken flocks past and present.

Patti Gordon, for showing me her lovely farm home, originally the setting for this book.

Brenda Mancini, Administrative Assistant at P.C.V.S., for details about Dr. H.R.H. Kenner, Principal at Peterborough Collegiate and Vocational School (1908–1943).

John Chesney B.A., outdoorsman and teacher for 35 years, who described visits of a student's pet crow to his classroom at Grove Public School in Peterborough.

Grietje R. McBride, B.Sc., teacher for 33 years, for very helpful detailed editorial suggestions in the beginning chapters of the text.

Robert C. McBride, B.Sc., M.Ed., a teacher, librarian, principal, and consultant in Gifted Education for 32 years, and now editor of the national magazine, The Loyalist Gazette. His enthusiasm, as one of my students many years ago and now as a reader of my books and this text in particular, has been most helpful. He has always been and still is a great source of encouragement.

Robert Bruce of Belleville, a retired O.P.P. officer who mapped the route for the journey from Massassaga to Lang at that time.

Dr. & Mrs. J. Sheppard, Peterborough neighbours, who visited an elderly doctor, to inquire regarding the medications used in the 1930s and before. Thanks especially to Liz who tabulated those notes for me.

Ann Featherstone, of Featherstone Editing Services, whose suggestions for cutting/adding to my story made all the difference in making it marketable, and

Christie Harkin, Editor of Children's Books, and Sharon Fitzhenry, Publisher of Fitzhenry & Whiteside, for their support and encouragement.

CONTENTS

ONE: BONNIE AND HER SHADOW

Bonnie awoke suddenly to strange sounds below her tiny bedroom. Jumping up, she crept out into the small hallway. She started down the steep pine stairs, still in her pyjamas. It was dark, but through the window in the front door below, she could see figures moving about the yard. She could hear her father's voice. Something was going on.

"Those two are hard-working beasts, but they're not used to long shifts. So I told Elvin not to push them. I'll be needing them to plant crops at the new place."

New place? Bonnie didn't know anything about a new place. Her heart sank. She loved it here in the Massassaga community, surrounded by stately maple trees and gentle fields of peas and tomatoes. But Father's crops had failed this year, and there was something called a *debt*. Her mother and father talked about it every night after supper—even while she was at the table.

She crept down the remaining stairs and opened the front door. Shadow would come. Beautiful, sleek, and black, he had a diamond-shaped white spot under his chin and another on the tip of his tail. Every night she would sneak out of bed to let him in. Then she'd smuggle him under her quilt and fall asleep to the sound of his contented purring.

"Shadow..." she whispered. "Shadow...come here!"

Something moved under the lilac bush. Good, there he was. He'd come toward the door in a moment, maybe once

1

things quieted down a bit.

"Good thing Elvin left here with time enough to get your wagon through Belleville this morning before too many other wagons and cars were moving about." It was Grandpa O'Carr, her mum's father. What was he doing here in the middle of the night?

"Hopefully, with a full-day's head start, we'll get our farm supplies to the new place just after we get through with the rest. And I was careful not to overload the wagon."

"I hope the daytime traffic didn't spook the horses too much," said Grandpa. "Those motor cars would startle the steadiest horse."

"They're the way of the future. Soon there won't be a horse left on any farm," said Dad.

"You and your new-fangled machinery," grumbled Grandpa. "You think you can push a button and get all your farming done before noon!"

"By George, a bit of good machinery would help. But I can't afford it."

"Humph. You'll never get machinery shipped that far north, anyway!"

"It's not that far!" Dad protested. "We'll have a beautiful brick home with a small orchard and a garden...and the rent is very reasonable."

"That may be, but in those parts! The land will be hard to till; it's full of hills and rocks—like the ones you've got in your head for picking that place."

Bonnie could hear low mumbling and shuffling coming

2

from the kitchen. Uncle Adam and Uncle Marsh emerged, lugging a huge box. So Dad's brothers were here, too. It was practically a family reunion! And they had put her to bed to sleep through it all.

Bonnie stepped out and crouched behind the cedar bush till her uncles had passed by. Then the moon shone out from behind a cloud. Now she could see her way around to look for Shadow. She whispered in a low voice, "Shadow! C'mon, Shadow!"

The September night was cool but she didn't care if she caught a cold. Was this really going to be her last night at home? She must find Shadow. They would need to stick together. Would that new place be as bad as Grandpa O'Carr said?

Bonnie and her Shadow. Dad had thought of both names. Beatrice was Bonnie's real name, and Mum wanted to call her Bea. "She'll be my little helper," she'd said. "Busy as a bee, just like her mother." But Dad had won out. At first sight of the baby in the cradle, he'd declared she was a bonnie lass, and so all the Browns called her Bonnie. Soon everyone did.

"You know, there's no call to be moving out of your home— lock, stock, and barrel—in the middle of the night." Grandpa's voice boomed out over the dooryard as men carried the dining-room table to Uncle Adam's cattle truck. Bonnie could hear the cows shuffling and mooing. Was the good furniture going to be packed right next to the cows? She hoped they had a partition between them. "I bought those things when you married my daughter and I still have the receipts. By law, they belong to me. It's a real shame that you're losing your farm because you can't meet those mortgage payments, but I'll see you don't lose anything else. They'll not get their hands on your beds and tables. They're mine."

"Are you sure?" Dad sounded worried. "What about the tax collectors?"

"My taxes are paid, so the same holds true," said Grandpa. "I won't let anyone take away your furniture."

"Well, I'm glad someone's doing well."

"It's not your fault, son. It's this miserable Depression. And it can't last forever."

"I thought it'd be over by now. But 1936 has been no better than the first half of this decade." To Bonnie's surprise, her tough old Grandpa O'Carr put out his hand and patted her father on the shoulder.

The wind whipped clouds back over the moon. Nearby crickets chirped loudly. Everything suddenly went dark again. Then she heard the sound of a big truck screeching to a quick stop on the highway right in front of their house.

"You bloomin' idiot!" Dad's voice came through the other night sounds.

Bonnie jumped up from behind the cedar bush She shook off some broken twigs and took a few steps toward her father. He didn't see her. He was staring at the truck and shouting, "Can't you watch where you're going? Now just look what you've done!"

The driver jumped out of the cattle truck parked on the other side of the road and looked under his front wheel. "I didn't see the cat there! Honest!" Dad crossed over the highway and held his lantern close. Both men were now staring down.

With a gasp, Bonnie ran toward the road.

"Stop!" Dad yelled at Bonnie as she dashed ahead. He met her halfway across the road and pulled her back to their front dooryard with his strong arms. "No use you looking now, Bonnie," he said. "That little mite's gone to heaven for sure."

"But he's under the truck!"

"Bonnie, what are you doing out there?" Mum's sharp voice cut through the damp night air. Bonnie started to cough. Her mother ran outside and, grabbing her daughter's hand, led her back into the house and over to sit in the wooden rocking chair by the kitchen door. Lantern light glowed around the chair, but the corners of the empty room were full of dark shadows. Boxes stood piled by the doorway.

Mum took a thick quilt and threw it over Bonnie. Its green and reddish-blue patches seemed to glow in the light of the lantern. Bonnie started crying.

Dad followed them inside and knelt beside his daughter. "Bonnie, I'm sorry—I'll get you another cat."

"I don't want another one!" Bonnie wailed. "I want Shadow. Now he's dead! I hate that man!"

"No one can see in the dark," said Dad. "The cat should have been sleeping in the barn. No one knew he was heading for the house."

A sudden realization hit Bonnie in the stomach like a fist. She was the one who let Shadow into the house at night. Now she couldn't stop the tears rolling down her cheeks.

5

"Come, mop up those tears. Let me see those big blue eyes again," said Dad, handing Bonnie his big red kerchief. "It's too bad. Poor Shadow would have been just fine at our new place. No cars for miles."

"No cars for miles!" Bonnie gasped. "Where are we going? To the North Pole?"

"Only about seventy miles north. We're moving to a fine farm between Lang and Keene—about twelve miles from Peterborough," said Dad. "It'll be a big adventure. You'll see."

"But I don't know that place," said Bonnie. "I like it right here in Massassaga. I like going to Belleville with Grandma Brown. Peterborough's too far away."

"We're going to miss our relatives, all right," said Mum. "But it'll have its compensations. Your uncles won't be snitching my pies and cakes out of the pantry window before they've even cooled down." Then she smiled at Dad, for Mum was a crackerjack cook, and she was just bragging a bit about everyone going for her baking.

Bonnie wasn't just sad now—she was angry. "I don't want to leave Grandma and Grandpa Brown!" she stormed. "I don't want to leave my school! I like my school. Miss Anderson said I could take Grades Four and Five together this year. I will *not* move!"

She stood up and stamped one foot on the floor.

"We'll see about that, young lady," said Mum. "Get into some warmer clothes now. And calm down or you'll bring on another coughing attack!"

Bonnie looked at her father with pleading eyes.

"It can't be helped, Bonnie. Now, do as your mother says. I have work to finish up." He bent over, kissed her on the forehead, and hurried out the door.

"Go back to your bedroom, Bonnie," said Mum. "I've laid out your skirt and blouse. Since you're up anyway, you might as well put them on and wait there. We'll call you when we're ready to go."

Bonnie wished they would forget her. She trudged across the dining room into the hallway and up the steep stairs. She hadn't had a chance to say goodbye to anyone—not her teacher nor her school friends. And not even her Grandma Brown or her aunts who lived in the big house on the hill next door. Nor Grandma O'Carr and Aunt Leah, who lived on the Ridge Road near Stirling—nineteen miles north of Belleville.

She was going to hate this new place. She knew it. Perhaps she wouldn't have to go. Maybe Mum and Dad *would* forget her. They were always busy working anyway. Bonnie put her clothes on quickly and flung herself on the little cot in her room.

Shadow. If only he were coming too. She wouldn't have been quite so lonesome. Then she buried her face in her pillow and sobbed for her cat, her school friends, her aunts and uncles, her grandparents—just everyone. And whatever would the new home be like? *Would* there be polar bears and icebergs away up north?

Later, someone covered her, half asleep, with a blanket and wedged her between piles of boxes in the back seat of the car.

****

She was floating on a leaky raft in the middle of Lake Ontario. Dad had told her to leave the farm and go to the North Pole. But she was lost. She couldn't even see the sandy banks of the shoreline. Clinging to the raft, she rode up and down the huge waves.

When she woke up, she was lying on a bare mattress on top of a table in a strange room.

"Where's Dad?" Bonnie asked her mum, who was now busy unpacking one of the utility cupboards by the light of a coal-oil lamp.

"Oh, he'll be here soon. He brought us and all the breakables in the car first. After he helped unload the cattle truck, he went back with the driver."

"Without us?"

"He just went along to meet your uncle with the horses. Your dad is driving them here now while Elvin goes home with the truck driver. It's been a long walk for those horses today. They set out early yesterday and now here it is, coming on three a.m.; so your dad'll have to take this last stretch pretty slowly. Still, he'll be along soon."

Just then a faint melody broke the silence.

"...she'll be comin' round the mountain when she comes! She'll be ridin' six white horses when she comes..." It was Dad, singing that silly song that Mum disliked.

But her mother looked happy. She rushed to throw open the front door. It was only a few feet from Bonnie's table-bed.

He'd found his way safely over the dark countryside and was
coming across the field.

Bonnie lay back on her pillow and was soon sound asleep
again.

TWO: NEW NEIGHBOURS

The late-September light filtered through the north window and woke Bonnie up from her second sleep. The nightmares were gone. She could hear the sound of blue jays squabbling beyond the yard. She tumbled off her table-bed and weaved her way between stacked furniture and boxes over to the window to investigate. Father had said there would be a small apple orchard, a garden, and a splendid grassy dooryard.

Only two scraggly apple trees were in sight. Nothing like the beautiful orchards in Prince Edward County! The lawn was a mess of goldenrod and wild grass. The grass was so long in some places, it waved in the breeze. Bonnie turned her back on the window and pressed down her wrinkled navy blue skirt and white blouse. She hated her warm wool stockings. They were so furry looking. No one but Bonnie had to wear long wool stockings this early, but her mother was always afraid she would "take a chill." She scratched one leg and sighed.

"You strip that side and I'll do this side," came a strange voice from another room.

"Fine, Mrs. Elmhirst, I'll do that," said Mum. "I'm glad Bonnie's having a good long sleep. It was a tough night, and I'd rather not have her wandering in before we finish this room. She's always been a curious child. I don't want her to pick up any germs."

"Don't worry, Amy. This Lysol kills germs. And we'll be

10

through here by noon. Now put lots of Lysol on the wall after you tear off that wallpaper. Don't forget," the woman continued, "I cleaned out the pantry, too, after I finished the front room for your furniture. So now you'll have somewhere to put your dishes and food."

Food! Suddenly Bonnie realized how hungry she was. She slid around the boxes and old orange crates filled with their stuff, but the doorway was blocked with two mattresses. So she squeezed her head between them and shouted, "Mum!"

"Get back! Get out of here! At once!"

"Why?"

Her mother rushed over toward Bonnie like a bat flying out of a cave. "Don't contradict," she whispered. "Just get out to the verandah where there aren't any germs!"

"Why would there be germs?"

"The Elmh—" Mum hesitated, pushing her thick wavy hair out of her eyes. "The house has been empty for three years. That's all."

Bonnie shrugged and went looking for the front door. It would take a while to find it with all this furniture in the way. She walked through the tunnels between the piles of boxes and chairs and came to a small winding pathway of polished pine floor that led to the front door. For a minute, she thought she saw Shadow coming around the corner of one of the boxes. Then she remembered with a cold jolt: Of course, it couldn't be Shadow. Bonnie gulped back a sob and determined to explore some more. She mustn't think of Shadow right now.

Out on the verandah, the air was fresh and the sun shone

just the way it used to in Massassaga. Bonnie raced down the steps and through the overgrown grass.

She flung herself on the bushy lawn and gazed back at the big, red-brick house. It was much grander than their old grey clapboard home. One side was square but the other side was set back a bit, with a gable on the roof. A white picket fence and a verandah with gingerbread trim both wrapped around the house. It was strange that no one had wanted to rent it for three years. What was wrong with the place?

The blue jays were still making a ruckus in a tree just behind her. Bonnie sat up and turned around to get a better look. Now she saw the big long trail across a wide field. She got up and stepped over to the white picket fence. She squinted but couldn't see the road or any mailbox, though she supposed they had one. Then she looked to her left across the barnyard to the end of a hilly lane. She could only see as far as the top of the first hill. She was almost sure she saw something else—a boy walking along the rail fence up there. He was holding a long, willowy tree branch like a flagpole.

"Bonnie! Bonnie!"

She scrambled back to the house. There was no use hiding from her mother. She always found you—and she always had another job for you.

Well, I might as well get it over with, Bonnie thought.

So Bonnie clambered up the verandah steps and faced her mother.

"I don't have time to repeat myself, so listen carefully. I can't cook porridge because the stove isn't hooked up yet to the

12

stovepipes. But your grandmother packed sandwiches, and they're somewhere out here on the verandah in a cardboard box marked 'Food.' Eat first, then bring the rest inside for me and Mrs. Elmhirst."

"Who is Mrs. Elmhirst?"

"A very important lady who's helping us. Now, get going!"

Bonnie tiptoed along the verandah, looking at every box. Nothing there. So she tiptoed back and glanced over her shoulder at the row of bushes growing directly in front of the verandah. Was it possible that a box may have fallen somewhere between a bush and the verandah?

A spruce tree, just a little bigger than the others, stood right in front of her. She stopped to touch a bright green branch but quickly drew back her hand with a piercing shriek.

A long, thin green snake was draped over its branches just like Christmas tinsel.

"What's the matter, Bonnie?" It was Dad. He smelled like horses and cows.

"Snnnaa...Snnn aaaa..."

"What?"

"SNAKE! LOOK!"

Bonnie pointed at the spruce tree, but the reptile had slithered away.

"There's no snake there now. Besides, we have more important things to worry about than a small, harmless garter—like dirty barns." Dad grinned ruefully. As he clapped his hands against his overall legs, clouds of dust swirled around him.

Bonnie sneezed. "Boy! Everything's dirty around here," she said, "especially you. You have cobwebs all over your hair." She ran her hands through her own mop of short, curly blonde hair—a mess of tangles still not combed out this morning.

Her father was over six feet tall, and he towered above her, laughing. She hadn't seen him smile all summer. "You're completely right, Bonnie. It's a dirty place. And I have cobwebs for hair. But the price is right—and this wonderful farm will help us climb out of debt."

"If we don't starve first."

"Why on earth do you say that?"

"Because I can't find the lunch Grandma O'Carr made for us!"

"You're standing right in front of it."

Bonnie turned around and sure enough, there was the box marked "Food"—peeking out from behind the open front door.

Bonnie smiled and pulled brown paper lunch bags out of the wooden box. "Mum told me to eat first and then take some in to her and Mrs. Elmhirst. Now you and I can eat together!" Bonnie loved eating with just her father.

They sat down comfortably on the front steps. "So who is that lady who's putting Lysol all over everything?" asked Bonnie before biting into a generous piece of fresh homemade bread folded around a thick slice of pork with Grandma's own mustard. Her Grandma O'Carr's pork roast was always the best!

"Well," said Dad, biting into his own sandwich, "she's a

very special lady who has had a hard life. Her husband and daughter both got sick and she took care of them in this house. They died, but she has two sons who are still alive. One is in a sanitarium for patients with consumption. The doctors call it *tuberculosis* now, and there are new treatments these days. Anyway, the other son is quite well."

So that was the reason her mother and Mrs. Elmhirst were scrubbing so hard—to clean out the consumption germs. Bonnie gulped down her mouthful and then said, "Where does Mrs. Elmhirst live now?"

"She lives with her son, Roy, in Toronto—the one who's well."

"Why doesn't he run the farm?"

"Well, he has a good secretarial job in Toronto."

"I wonder how he managed to get that sort of job!"

"It wasn't easy. His mother ran this farm all by herself while she was taking care of her sick family. She had enough money to send Roy to business college, and he went on from there. He's a bachelor and his mother lives with him now. She is very proud of him."

"I would be proud of him, too!"

"Yes, and we're proud to be renting her farm. *No* talk about germs when you meet her, understand?" Bonnie turned to go but Dad grabbed the back of her collar and tipped her toward him. "Wait just a minute," he said. "Do you understand?"

Bonnie loved her father but every so often he could be very tough. And she did not like that. She squinted her eyes into slits. "Okay, Dad. But I don't—"

15

"No 'buts' about it. You button that lip and say nothing but 'How do you do, Mrs. Elmhirst. Pleased to meet you.'"

"But won't *we* get consumption?"

"No. It's been some years since they left the house and our doctor says it's ridiculous to think we can get it now after all that time."

"I see."

"The problem is that many folks are so afraid of the consumption that they have stupid fears. That's the reason that no one's rented this fine place till now. It's been vacant for the last three years."

"Okay. I'll be nice."

"That's my girl," said Dad, loosening his hold. "Now let's take some grub in to the ladies. We'll go in the back way."

Bonnie followed her father to one side of the verandah and along the short stone pathway to a shed made of wooden logs. "Next summer, we'll use this for our kitchen," said Dad, sizing up the place as they stepped through the doorway. "We'll set up our stove out here. Look, Bonnie, it has its own ventilation." Father pointed to the cracks where the chinking had fallen out between the logs.

Bonnie put her face right up against one of the cracks and looked back up the lane where she'd seen the boy with the aspen branch. There he was again! But he was going the opposite way this time—probably going home. Bonnie was a little disappointed.

"Who's that boy walking along the rail fence at the top of our lane, Dad?"

Her father came over and peered through the crack. "I don't know, but I saw him out there earlier. He must live in the neighbourhood."

"I hope he comes to visit," said Bonnie, following her father through the back door into the main house.

* * * *

The next morning, Bonnie stepped cautiously across the dooryard, through the gate, and into the barnyard. She was returning from helping her father send the cows out to pasture, but she didn't want her mother to notice her. After all, she still had lots of exploring to do. Bonnie looked toward the lane and there was the boy again, carrying another aspen branch. This time he was coming down the steep hill to the edge of their barnyard. And behind him, there were two other figures.

Bonnie ran helter-skelter across the barnyard and pulled open the heavy gate at the foot of the lane. The boy must have spotted her, for he seemed to be coming on—and Bonnie could see two older girls behind the branch.

"Hi," said the boy, as they drew up close. "What's your name?" He brushed back his white-gold hair and smiled at Bonnie.

"I'm Bonnie Brown. We just moved in."

"I know," said the boy.

"That's Archie, and I'm his sister, Angela. We're the Johnsons," said the taller, dark-haired girl. Her eyes were kind. "How old are you?"

"Nine," answered Bonnie, suddenly shy.

"I'm eleven," answered Angela, "like Marianne Hubbs, here."

The second girl bounced up and down as though she were jumping over an invisible skipping rope. Marianne looked like someone who could get into lots of mischief. But her big, friendly smile made Bonnie think she might make a good friend.

"We live on the two farms on the other side of your place," said Angela, sweeping her arm to the west.

"Yup!" said Marianne. "So, why did your folks—"

"Marianne!" said Angela. She shot her friend a warning look. Marianne snapped her mouth shut.

There was an awkward silence.

"I can guess what you're talking about," said Bonnie.

"Yeah," said Archie, wrinkling his nose and squishing up his freckled cheeks. Bonnie figured he must be at least a year younger than she was. "Aren't you afraid to live in that house? Jeepers! Two people died in there!"

"Well, my mother's disinfecting the house with Lysol right this very minute. That's supposed to take care of all the germs. Mind you, she always keeps her house spotless." Bonnie rolled her eyes up to the cloudless sky in disgust. "My uncles always say you can eat off her floors, they're so clean. I won't be so spotless when I grow up."

"Me, neither." Archie nodded sympathetically.

"Do you want to come up to the house and see inside?"

Bonnie invited.

The three children looked at each other cautiously.

Archie grinned. "Hey, that's why we're here!"

"We'd have come sooner," said Marianne. "But yesterday was my piano lesson. Mother teaches me. Golly! What I have to put up with! That practicing goes on forever."

"She's the youngest in the family and so her older sisters do most of the chores," said Archie. "But in my family, I'm the only boy. So I have to do lots of work for Dad."

"Well, I'm an only child," said Bonnie. "So I do chores for both my parents." That was partly true—but Mum kept her busy indoors, mostly.

"Well, maybe we should visit another day," said Angela. "Your mother might not want visitors this soon."

"Maybe you're right," Bonnie said casually.

"I guess we'd best skedaddle, then," said Archie.

Bonnie was sad, but a little relieved, too. She would have loved to invite her new friends to come inside the house. But Mum was definitely too busy for visitors.

THREE: THE LAW

"What's for breakfast today?" Bonnie asked. Of course, it would be the same porridge, but then there might be a spoonful of Grandma O'Carr's strawberry preserves. She plunked herself down on a chair in the dining room. That was what Mum had named this room, but really, it was the only downstairs room that they would live in until next spring. The parlour, where they'd packed away the lovely green-and-brown furry chesterfield and chair that Grandpa O'Carr had bought Mum, was much too cold.

The only heat in the house this winter would be coming from their old kitchen stove, which her parents had just hooked up this morning. Their old house hadn't had a furnace in the cellar either, but both her grandparents' houses had one. It was wonderful to have a furnace, for it heated all the rooms and made even the bedrooms warm.

"Just porridge and turnips," said Mum as she held the pan above Bonnie's plate.

Bonnie groaned. "Is there *anything* else?"

"Bonnie! No more talk like that!" said Mum sharply. "You'd better get used to it because that's all we're likely to have all winter." Mum gave a grunt of disgust as she set the pan in the warming oven above the stove.

"How about potatoes? And all those peas and tomatoes from back home in Massassaga?"

"The potato crop failed. Remember? And the peas and

tomato crops were poor, too. We sold what we could and put the money toward our debts. We are very fortunate to have so many turnips, at least."

"But we had lots and lots of McIntosh apples! That was a good crop this year."

"Yes," said Dad, carefully hooking wire around the now hot stovepipe to secure it where it ran along the ceiling, "but we had to sell most of them to pay for our move, and we have to keep some money back to cover vet bills if the cows get sick this winter."

Dad stepped off the stool and set the hammer and wire on the edge of the table. "You know, Bonnie, our ancestors went through a much rougher time—the hungry year! They'd have been *thankful* for turnips. In the spring, they even ate the buds off certain trees!"

Bonnie knew she'd better not say anymore. Her Loyalist ancestors had nearly starved in 1787. She'd heard about the story before. But that didn't stop her from thinking horrible thoughts. What *would* they be eating come spring?

Brrr-iiing, Brrr-brrr!

Bonnie leapt from her chair in fright.

Brrr-iiing, Brrr-brrr!

"What is that?" Bonnie asked. It sounded like an angry, oversized bullfrog.

"It's our telephone." Dad beamed. "And it's our ring—a long and two shorts!"

"A telephone!" exclaimed Bonnie with delight. She had always wanted to talk on one. But who would phone them out here?

Bonnie followed her father to the big telephone high up on the wall right beside the front window. It was a foot-high wooden box with two shiny bells at the top. There was a mouthpiece just below the bells and an earpiece in a holder on its left side.

"Browns' residence," said Dad, as if they lived in a palace.

Bonnie rolled her eyes. If only the caller could see all the packing boxes and the half–hooked-up stove! Then they wouldn't think too much of the Browns' "residence." A cough tickled her throat and burst out, dry and hacking.

"Sshhhh, Bonnie!" Mum hissed from behind her. "Do you want folks to think you've caught consumption already?"

"By George!" Dad said. "That'll be great. Count me in."

A low mumble came through the earpiece but even close by, Bonnie could not make out the words.

"Right, I'll meet you before long at the...Well, at the...you know."

What was Dad plotting? Bonnie wondered.

"Well, what was that all about, Thomas?" Mum said sternly from beside the stove.

"Oh, I've just hatched a little plan with our next-door neighbour, Herb Johnson."

"What kind of a plan?" said Mum, reaching for the poker behind the stove.

"We're going fishing."

"Fishing?" Mum's brown eyes opened wide in alarm. "That's illegal. It's not fishing season."

"I know that, Amy. But we have no meat to eat this winter—

22

not even a chicken's neck to wring."

Bonnie looked hopefully at her father. She wasn't so sure she liked fish, but it would be better than turnips.

"I hope the game warden wasn't listening in. It's a party line, you know."

"Yes, but we talked the details over before. So I just needed the go-ahead now."

"Well, I thought you said plenty. And if you're thrown in jail, what will Bonnie and I do?"

"Go home to your parents. They'll not put you out," said Dad. His clear blue eyes twinkled. He seemed to know what his wife's reaction would be to this suggestion.

"I'd sooner starve than go crawling home!"

"Well, you could always go on Relief. That'd pay the basics."

"Stop! Stop!" Mum hissed—something like a snake, thought Bonnie. She shuddered as she remembered the long snake on the little spruce tree.

"I'm not in this alone," Dad said. "Johnson and Post and Hubbs cooked up this scheme."

"Sure—and you'll go to jail together. Or more likely alone. You won't be able to pay the fine. They probably can."

"Don't worry so much, Amy. The game warden seldom works on Saturdays, and besides, they leave someone as a lookout. I'll slip right out of there if there's any sign of the law."

Mum finished poking the fire and then banged the poker onto its hook behind the stove. "Well, I'm not comfortable with this. So far we've always trusted God to provide."

"Yes, I agree, but we have to do our part. 'Look to the ant, thou sluggard. Consider her ways and be wise,'" quoted Dad.

Mum harrumphed. "I can't stop you—just hope you can outrun the warden."

Dad turned to Bonnie. "Want to come along?"

"Thomas, are you out of your mind?" said Mum. But Dad had already disappeared out the back door.

Bonnie followed and grabbed her old, blue knitted sweater and her black rubber boots from the back shed. Sitting on the steps just outside, she threw her old shoes off and pulled the tall boots on. Since she was short, the boots reached up to three inches above her knees. Then she pulled on the sweater and rushed, boots flapping, to catch up to her father.

She ran along the pathway to the small gate and into the barnyard. Just then, Dad came out of the granary with two empty sacks flung over his left shoulder. "C'mon, Bonnie," he said. "Keep up or stay at home." He swung back the long, heavy gate that separated the barnyard from the laneway leading toward the western boundary of the farm. It veered over steep hills until it reached a woodland of oaks and maple trees. Then it sloped down steeply to the main road that went south and west into the hamlet of Lang.

"Are we going to walk?" Bonnie asked.

"Of course. It's not worth taking the horses. Burnham's Dam is just a bit to the southwest. We'll be fishing in Indian River—the same one that runs through Lang."

Bonnie was concentrating so hard on keeping up with her father's long strides, she could hardly hear him. She was puffing just to keep breathing. Just last year, she'd been away from school for six weeks with a sore throat and swollen glands. Since then, she had never completely lost her cough. But Bonnie didn't let that ruin her day. She was so happy to be out in the fields on this crisp day in early fall. It was much better than being stuck in a house that smelled so strongly of Lysol.

Bonnie and her father left the hilly laneway and headed across the steep fields. Before long, they arrived at a rail fence. Dad climbed over and strode on across the grassy field on the other side of the fence. "I'm going to be ploughing this field next week. Hope I get all the ground worked up before snowfall. It's plenty hard. Wouldn't it be great if I could just push a button on a machine, and it would plough the fields in no time at all?"

"Is that why Mum and Uncle Elvin call you 'push-a-button,' sometimes?"

Dad laughed. "I guess so."

"Then you could plough more fields and plant more crops. For sure, we wouldn't be in debt then," said Bonnie, sliding easily between the rails. She plodded across the meadow behind her father and down a grassy hill, stepping in and out of his shadow. Then Bonnie looked up and saw one of their four black-and-white cows grazing in the sunny, green meadow. The others were lying under the tall maples.

"There are those cows, lazing around as usual!" said Bonnie. "All they ever do is sleep, and all we ever do is work!"

"That's right," said Dad, "and starting tomorrow morning, you'll be bringing in those cows every morning for milking.

I'll wake you up at six o'clock."

Bonnie gasped. "But, Dad, I—"

"I don't have your Uncle Marsh or your Uncle Adam anymore. So you are going to do your share, young lady. You'll get the cows every morning and every night till the snow flies. Then they'll stay in the barn or barnyard."

Bonnie grimaced. She wondered what Mum would say about Bonnie's new chore. After all, Mum made her work inside the house most of the time, where she didn't have a chance to daydream. And she'd probably worry about Bonnie catching colds in the damp morning air.

They'd come to the edge of their farm. On the other side of the rail fence, beyond the road, was a thick woodland.

"Now, Bonnie," said Dad, "the river is in the middle of those woods. Take a good look at where you are." Bonnie stared straight ahead. "Now, turn around and stare back across our fields and up that big hill. Our laneway's on the other side."

Bonnie did as she was told, although she could not see the lane let alone the house.

"So, do you think you could find your way home from here?"

"I...think...so."

"Well, we'll be walking straight south down this road for a mile or so. After the fishing, we'll walk straight back up this road to our property. Now, remember that."

"Oh, I'll be fine," said Bonnie, even though she didn't feel fine.

Dad continued. "If you get lost, just keep on going and

you'll come out on one of those roads to the north or west of the woods. See how the road winds around?"

"Yes, I do, but why don't I come back with you?"

"I hope we can come back together. I'm just telling you in case..."

"In case of what?"

"Nothing much, but if the game warden comes by, I'll have to skedaddle. You might have to make your own way home since I'll not be waiting for you. C'mon. I've wasted enough time."

Dad put both hands on top of the fence and flung his legs over it, landing lightly on the other side without even dropping his fishing rod. Bonnie was having a harder time struggling through between the rails. These ones had rough spots that ripped across one of her rubber boots. She was glad it had not torn.

It soon seemed to Bonnie that she and Dad had been walking along the dusty road for hours and hours. Bonnie took three steps to each one of her father's. Her shiny black rubber boots made it harder to keep up because they were heavy. She almost wished she hadn't worn them, but she sure wasn't going to miss this chance of wading in the river. Her rubber boots were perfect for that. She could hardly wait.

Then her father walked into a ditch full of grass that was almost as tall as Bonnie. She parted the blades in front of her and saw her father disappearing into the pine and poplar trees ahead.

Bonnie tried to speed up but, without warning, she

sprawled over an old gnarled root that ran across the little pathway.

"Wait!" Bonnie screamed.

Her father turned around. "Are you all right, Bonnie?" He walked back and pulled her up on her feet. "You've got to keep quiet."

Her hands were dirty and a bit bloody, but the scrapes were not deep. So Bonnie said, "Sorry, Dad. I'm just fine." She brushed off her palms and then her overalls. She'd never yell again on this trip—not even if she saw a bear or a wolf or anything else. She'd show Dad that she was brave.

But it was almost impossible to stop being clumsy. Her mother always told her how clumsy she was. Mum was right. No matter how hard Bonnie tried to walk carefully, she was forever falling over her own feet. The boots just made it worse. Actually, her mother thought Dad was clumsy, too. It was true that Mum was much handier at repairing things around the house and barn. Bonnie felt certain she must have inherited all the clumsy parts of Dad and none of the strong, graceful parts of her mother.

She looked up again and saw that Dad was far ahead of her on the trail. She began to run, being very careful to avoid tree roots. She caught up to him in a small clearing that led to a river and a low dam.

"Well, here we are, Bonnie. This is Burnham's Dam."

Bonnie walked toward the edge of Indian River and put her hands on her hips. So, Bonnie and Dad had made it to the river. Now she'd go wading. She would make good use of these new boots!

"Not so fast, young lass!" came a strong but quiet voice from behind her.

She turned and looked back at a pair of the darkest, bushiest eyebrows she'd ever seen. They were attached to Mr. Johnson, Archie and Angela's father.

"Better stay away from the river's edge," Mr. Johnson said quietly. "We're wanting to catch fish. We don't want to end up fishing you out!"

Bonnie moved away from the riverbank and watched the water rush over the dam. It foamed up when it hit the river below and Bonnie knew that the foam was probably hiding lots of fish. A few men had cast nets there.

"Good to see you, Brown," said Mr. Johnson, raising his bushy eyebrows and smiling. "The suckers are thick here today. No one will need to go hungry this winter. Forget about that fishing rod and bait," he added, as Dad set his rod down on the ground and took a bottle of worms out of his inside coat pocket. "It'll be too slow. If the nets fail, we'll use our spears. We'll have our sacks full in no time."

Now it was Dad's turn to smile. Bonnie liked seeing him do that—mostly because he almost always looked sad and worried.

"This here's your neighbour Post, and over there is Hubbs," Mr. Johnson was saying.

Mr. Post was a short, jolly man. He beamed a big smile at Dad out from under his red hair.

Bonnie followed the men down to the water. Then she

looked out past the river to the spruce and cedar bush on the opposite side. This north country did look scraggly, but the air was crisp and the sky looked as blue as any day in Massassaga. While they sorted out the nets, she watched some fish slip out of the water, then tumble over the falls.

"Oh, Dad, look at that big one!" she cried out.

"Bonnie!" Dad growled. "If you can't be quiet, go back in the bush. The fish will hear you and they'll all be scared away!"

"Either that or you'll bring on the law!" laughed Mr. Johnson. Then he added quietly, "Don't worry, Brown. I've left Archie back to watch. He'll whistle if he sees the game warden. And anyway, with these fish jumping into our big nets, we'll be out of here in a quarter of an hour—tops!"

So Archie was here! Would she be able to spot him from the river's edge back at the top of the dam?

Bonnie trudged through the underbrush of poplar saplings and fallen cedar logs and scrambled up to the higher ground. There, not too far away, was a white-blond–haired boy looking straight at her.

FOUR: FISH BALLS

Bonnie tramped over the ground's thick coat of fallen leaves, waving to her neighbour.

"Hey! I'm glad you've come," Archie said, once Bonnie had managed to cross over to him. "It's lots of fun helping out here. And it would be even better if we got to miss school for it."

"You don't like school?"

"It's not so bad now that I'm older, but it's sure boring."

"How old are you?"

"I turned eight last March."

Bonnie grinned. "I'm older than you. I turned nine in August. But we can still be friends. I've always wanted a little brother."

"Little! Jeepers! You're not much bigger than I am." Archie laughed, then made a face. "Anyway, I already have two older sisters. You met Angela, and the oldest one is Lizzie. Then there's my baby sister Teenie."

"Any brothers?"

"Nope. I wish I had one. There's only my father and me to do all the farm work. I tell you, there's no way I'm going to be a farmer when I grow up. I'm going to be a soldier, just like my Dad was in the Great War." Archie saluted a nearby poplar tree and braced himself against the autumn wind that had begun rifling through the woods.

"You're crazy!" Bonnie said. "I'd like to play a game."

"We could play jacks," said Archie. "Here, these pebbles

would work just fine."

"Do you have a ball?" Bonnie asked.

"'Fraid I don't. I'd have to make one."

"Well, let's not bother. I'd sooner play I SPY."

"Okay, but, jeepers, that's a kind of boring game."

"I spy something that's blue and white," said Bonnie.

"Nothing like that in the middle of these woods!" said Archie. "So give me another clue."

"It's high up," said Bonnie.

"Can you really see a cloud up there?" asked Archie, stretching his neck to peer straight upward. "I can't."

Bonnie stared straight up too. "Well, I can't now but I did before. I really did, Archie. So it should count."

"Well, keep looking up and maybe it'll roll over the treetops again." Staring straight up, they waited.

"Well, isn't this quaint," said a nasty voice from behind them. A big man with a brown jacket grabbed Archie by the back of his collar. Struggling, Archie put a whistle to his lips and blew it hard. The man grabbed Archie's whistle.

"Hey, you! Give me back my property!" Archie shouted.

"Trying to warn your friends, I see! Well, you don't fool me." The man threw Archie into a patch of prickly bushes and headed straight toward Burnham's Dam.

"Wait, Mister!" Bonnie shouted. She ran up beside the game warden and plunked her hands on her hips, staring up at the scowling, bearded face.

The game warden turned to her with a smirk. "And what do you have to say, snippet?"

"I'm new in these parts, and Archie was just showing me how to blow this whistle."

"He was, was he?"

"Yes, and we're talking about school. I'm going to Lang School, starting on Monday."

"I see. Do your parents know you two are out here in the woods?" He smirked at them again and said, "But of course they do. They've left you to watch for me."

"Oh, no, you've got it wrong," said Bonnie. "My parents have rented that farm yonder and I walked right to the end of the fields and down the road a piece. Then I saw Archie and came over to visit." Bonnie was standing in front of the man now—on the pathway between him and the dam.

"Are you from *that* farm? The Elmhirst farm?" The man looked in horror in the direction Bonnie had pointed. Then he started backing away from her. "Git away from me. Git back." He turned to look at Archie and shook his finger at him. "I'll get into that river another way. Don't you doubt that!" Then he pointed to Bonnie. "But I'm not going past that one. And you better steer clear, too, if you don't want to die by choking up your own blood. Have some sense, boy! Git away from her!"

Bonnie stared at the man for a moment, but then, bending over, she started to cough loudly. The man turned and disappeared back the way he had come.

Archie put his index finger and thumb together in his mouth and whistled sharply through his teeth. Then he did it a second time for full measure. When he'd caught his breath, he said, "That man's ignorant, he is. Mum says there's no need to worry anymore. The place is out of quarantine. C'mon." He grabbed Bonnie's hand. "We gotta warn the men. Maybe they didn't hear my signal." Together they ran the short distance through the thick woods to the river.

The men had heard Archie's whistling but only her Dad snuck out from behind a tree and then ran toward her with a bulging sack over each shoulder. "You know the way, Bonnie," he panted. "Head for home! I can't wait for you." He galloped on past, his long legs taking their full stride. The thick woods closed in around him.

A dark shadow seemed to pass over the woods, and Bonnie shivered.

Then, forgetting all about Archie, she plucked up her courage and ran headlong in the direction her father had run. As before, her clattering rubber boots held her back. She glanced down at them—and ran smack into a short spruce shrub.

Bonnie collapsed on the ground, bent her head over her lap, and gritted her teeth together. She'd never find her way out of these woods! But of course she would—she must! So she got up and started on again. Then she thought of Archie. Wherever had he gone?

"Bonnie! Bonnie!"

It was Archie! He was nearby. "Over here," she yelled back.

In a few minutes, Archie appeared next to the spruce shrub. "Hey! What are you doing?" he asked.

"I'm just…resting."

"Jeepers! You're closer to the river now. You need to go the opposite way to get to the main road."

"I guess I'm kind of turned around. Where's your farm from here?"

"Depends. The shorter way would be through these trees to the road and through the Hubbs' farm. The longer way 'round would take me by the road to the end of your farm."

"Come my way—please?"

"Sure!" Archie smiled. "And anyway, it's easier walking on the road than across ploughed fields."

Bonnie jumped up, ready to walk beside him.

"You just follow me," Archie said. "The underbrush is thick here, but I'll open up the way." He held back the prickly branches of a cedar bush that was blocking their way.

Bonnie followed her new friend. *Maybe Archie's lost, too,* she worried. They were surrounded by a thick undergrowth of green cedar and spruce. Yellow elm and orange maple leaves lay on the ground, but there were still plenty of oak leaves on the trees around them, making the woods very dark. When they finally reached the end of the woods, Bonnie could hardly believe her eyes. She was looking straight across the road at the edge of her family's farm. The rail fence was snaking along beside their four black-and-white cows that were still grazing near the maple trees. It looked as if nothing had happened.

"You'd better hurry home," said Archie. "Most likely your mother will want you to help her clean the suckers. Did you know that's all there is this time of year—suckers! They're awfully bony fish. So my mother and sisters will be busy all day putting them up."

At Bonnie's perplexed look, Archie explained, "Mum chops up the meat with the butcher knife and chugs it into glass jars. Then she pours in some sauce made of vinegar and salt and spices, and she screws the lids on tight."

Bonnie understood. "We call those jars 'sealers.' Mum does most of her preserves in sealers—but never fish. Don't suckers have to be cooked?"

"They cook inside the jars. Mum seals the full jars real tight and puts them into her copper washing kettle on top of the stove. Then she pours water in until the jars are covered. Then she boils the water."

Bonnie was dubious. "I don't think my mother would do all that for suckers," she said. "She doesn't even like the salmon and bass that Dad caught in Bay of Quinte back home. So why would she keep these old suckers? She'll cook up a few in our iron spider frying pan, but after we've all choked on the bones, she'll toss the rest away."

"Oh, the bones won't hurt you. After they're boiled in that vinegar, they go all soft. You won't know which is bones and which is sucker!"

"Eeuggh!"

"No, they're good!" Archie insisted. "Mum opens the jars up one at a time, adds flour, and then rolls the fish into little patties and fries them up. They taste almost like salmon balls!"

"Maybe that's not quite so bad."

"Just wait till you try it! Now I've got to head home. See you!"

"See you," said Bonnie, as she squeezed through the fence and started running up the hill. She wanted to get as far as she could while Archie was still in sight. As soon as she reached the top of the hill, she hoped she'd be able to see the barn and the house on the other side.

* * * *

"What good are these awful fish?" Mum was shouting.

Bonnie had just come running into their big all-purpose dining room. But she stopped short when she heard the angry voices coming from the backyard. She opened the back door and peeked out. Her parents were glaring at each other.

"It'll be food in our stomachs this winter. We don't have any meat."

"But I've never preserved fish! I don't even know if it's safe. We'll all die of poison."

"Oh, yes, it's safe," said Bonnie. Both parents looked at her, perplexed.

"What do you know about cooking?" Dad chuckled. It was no secret that Bonnie hated to cook and that her mother complained about anything Bonnie tried to make.

"I know all about preserving those suckers! Archie told me. His mother has a special recipe. They clean the fish and put them in sealers on the stove and boil them for hours—and the bones all soften and then they put them in the cold cellar all winter and they keep just fine." Dad was laughing now, but Mum was listening.

"Thomas, carry those sacks down to the cellar. Then we are going to visit our neighbours. I need that recipe right away."

* * * *

Duke and Rose lumbered up the hilly lane, pulling the wagon toward the road that led to the Johnsons' farm. Mum sat beside Dad on the high seat and Bonnie was perched behind him on a bag of grain. It was a bit windy in the open air, but Bonnie didn't mind. She was overjoyed to be visiting her new friends.

Dad let the horses fly up the hills, through the woods, and onto the road at the western edge of the farm. He turned north—not south toward Burnham's Dam. Then at the top of a steep, short hill, they looked down the sloping lane to a valley where a red brick house and a grey barn were sheltered by a line of spruce and basswood trees.

"Well, I do believe we've arrived," said Dad dreamily, gazing at a stand of poplars and tamaracks at the north end of the Johnsons' farm. "If it weren't for those hills, we would have been here even sooner. Too bad we couldn't have come in the car, but we've got to save that little bit of gasoline for an emergency."

"Well, Push-a-Button," Mum said. "The car certainly is a convenience we all miss—but how about we get these horses moving in the meantime? I must get that fish recipe!"

"Oh, yes, the suckers," said Dad. He loosened the horses' reins and the wagon started moving again. In minutes, they were in front of the Johnsons' place.

A short woman with light brown hair was standing on the big, rambling verandah, wiping her hands on a stiffly starched apron.

"Come right in. Unhitch the horses and stay for dinner!" said Mrs. Johnson with a big, friendly smile. Angela and her mother moved to either side of the front door, motioning the Browns to come in.

"We really can't just drop in on you unannounced!" said Mum. "I had no idea it was so near dinnertime." All farmers ate their big meal of the day at noon.

"I won't hear of you not staying, Amy. In you come! And Thomas—you and my husband will want to trade fish tales!"

The Browns walked into a well-scrubbed kitchen with braided rugs. To Bonnie, it looked like heaven with its cosy inside and all the friendly faces.

Mrs. Johnson tousled Bonnie's hair. "Don't you just look like Shirley Temple with those golden curls," she said.

"That's what everyone used to say back home!" Bonnie smiled. "And I've seen her, too, at the movies in *Poor Little Rich Girl* and *Heidi*!"

"When did you see those, Bonnie?" Mum asked. "We never go to movies."

Bonnie hesitated. "I went with Aunt Dollie."

"I thought she took you to the library," said Dad.

"We went there, too."

Bonnie smiled with relief as all the grownups burst out laughing. Then, as they were ushered to the table, she breathed in the smell of freshly baked bread and luscious apple pie. Beside the big, steaming bowls of potatoes and carrots, there were fresh chicken and dumplings and all kinds of pickles— sliced cucumbers made bread-and-butter style, beet pickles, and tiny whole cucumber pickles. Bonnie knew she shouldn't stare, but she couldn't help it.

Archie and Angela had joined them at the table, and their older sister Lizzie was there too. Lizzie was thirteen, and her blonde hair was drawn back in a grown-up way. At the opposite end of the room, their baby sister Teenie was throwing things on the floor—her spoon, bits of potato, and even some chicken. Bonnie could not imagine what her own mother would say if a baby did that to her spotless kitchen floor! But Mrs. Johnson kept patiently putting the spoon back in the baby's hand.

"So, Bonnie, are you coming to our school on Monday?" Archie blurted out, his mouth full of dumplings.

"Yes, and I can't wait! I love school!"

"You love school?" Archie stopped chewing and looked at Bonnie as if a spruce twig had just grown out of the top of her head.

"Close your mouth, Archie Johnson. No one wants to see your half-chewed dinner!" Lizzie scolded.

Bonnie swallowed quickly so she could answer Archie. "Yes, I do," she said. "And my teacher back home said I could do two grades together this year."

"Jeepers! You'll be stuck doing homework all the time. Too bad! I'm going to be on Tom and Slinky's baseball team."

"Who are Tom and Slinky?"

"Oh, they're the best baseball players in the school."

Bonnie wasn't really interested in baseball. Bonnie's mother had won a trophy for being top athlete in her school on Fair Day, but Bonnie felt like a complete stumblebum when it came to hitting things with bats and rackets. Baseball, tennis, badminton—whenever she saw something coming at her through the air, she ducked or whacked at it without looking.

"I love baseball season," said Archie, loading a spoonful of bread-and-butter pickles onto his plate. "I usually get picked about second or third."

"Really?" said Bonnie, trying to sound polite. "That must be nice."

"Yeah…I sure feel sorry for those bunglers who always get picked last."

Like me, Bonnie thought, twirling her fork through the creamed potatoes on her plate. She was beginning to get a bad feeling about starting school on Monday.

Mrs. Johnson stood up, her blue eyes twinkling. "Eat up, everyone—apple and pumpkin pie for dessert."

"Dessert!" Dad exclaimed, looking as if he had arrived in heaven. "We came for one recipe and you've given us a banquet."

"I love feeding people!" said Mrs. Johnson with a genuine smile.

"It's so nice to taste another woman's cooking. I get so tired of my own," said Mum. "Your dumplings are the lightest and tastiest I've ever had. I'll be so glad when I get some chickens."

"We could help you," said Mrs. Johnson, bringing two

41

pumpkin pies and one apple pie over to the table.

"Thank you, but we'll be fine. My father is bringing us his incubator and enough eggs. I'll hatch them this winter and we'll have a henhouse full next year at this time!" Mum helped herself to a slice of pie. "But when we've finished dinner, I would like that recipe for preserving fish. And I really must get right back before they spoil."

"Of course. I'd even come over to help you, but I have a boatload to do up myself and then there's the cleaning up afterward…. That seems to take even longer!"

"Well, I'm used to hard work," said Mum. Bonnie rolled her eyes to the ceiling, which made Archie smile.

"But you don't know about preserving suckers, Amy," said Mrs. Johnson. "Listen—why don't I send Lizzie home with you to help?"

After dinner, Mrs. Johnson refused to let Bonnie's mother help with the dishes. "Angela and I will manage just fine and you need to get back to the suckers," said Mrs. Johnson.

"Thank you so much for a lovely visit and a delicious dinner," said Mum. "And it's so kind of you, Alice, to send Lizzie to help me."

Then Dad got the wagon ready, and Bonnie and Lizzie climbed onto the back while Mum and Dad clambered onto the seat up front.

"Wait! You can't go yet!" shouted Archie as he pelted toward the barn. "I have something for you, Bonnie. You can't leave without it."

Archie soon rushed out of the barn and raced back. In his

arms, he held a furry golden pup. When he sat it on the ground, it started running around him in circles. It was a collie, just like the one Grandpa Brown had back in Massassaga.

"We've been training him to be a cow dog!" said Mr. Johnson. Archie picked up the pup and sat him beside Bonnie. The little fellow promptly jumped up, putting his two white paws on Bonnie's chest.

Startled, Bonnie fell back. "My goodness!" she exclaimed.

The pup jumped off the wagon and whimpered. Archie's face drooped into a look of utter disappointment. Then Bonnie looked down at the little puppy.

"You have all-white feet!" Bonnie smiled. "Just like boots!"

"Hey! You guessed his name!" Archie smiled, hopeful. "I call him Boots."

"We thought you might like a friend in your new place," said Angela. "He'll be good company."

"C'mon, Boots," said Bonnie. At the sound of her friendly tone, the little dog jumped toward the wagon. Archie lifted him up again. This time, Bonnie stroked the puppy's head. He had a white star just above his nose. "Well, I'll always miss my cat, but you're not bad—for a dog. Thank you, Archie."

"We can sure make good use of a dog. Collies always make fine cow dogs." Dad smiled as he and Mum turned around to look back at the little pup.

"But you'll have to take care of him, Bonnie," said Mum. "He'll need feeding, you know."

"Oh, sure," said Bonnie.

"I'll make a warm spot for him in the barn," said Dad.

Everyone knew that farm dogs lived outside and slept in the barn like all the other farm animals. Then Dad handed Mum the horses' reins while he came around back and tied a piece of binder twine around the dog's homemade leather collar and attached the other end of the twine to the front seat of the wagon. Boots whined a bit as they drove away and shuffled around to look for Archie. Bonnie stared at the lonely little fellow and at the sad look on Archie's face.

Suddenly, Bonnie knew just how the dog felt. She pulled him over to her side and stroked his back. Then he set his head on her lap and stretched his long nose across her knees. He lay very still and quiet as the wagon pulled out onto the road leading back to the farm.

Bonnie scratched and patted the white star on his forehead. The golden pup made a happy grunting sound. When she let her hand fall down beside him, he looked up at her with his big eyes and nudged her hand. Taking the hint, she stroked his head again. While Bonnie vowed never to forget Shadow, she could already tell that Boots was going to be a good friend.

FIVE: A ROUGH START

Out of the corner of her eye, Bonnie could see Dad scything down the tall yard-grass as she and Mum hurried out the front door. The sky was bright blue. It was the first Monday in October and a cool, gentle wind moved the branches of the maple trees west of the house. Boots ran in and out of the shade of the trees, happily chasing his tail. Bonnie was on her way to school.

Mum tugged at her hand. "Hurry up, child, I don't have all day."

"I could go to school with Archie and Angela. Why don't you drop me off there?"

"Because I have to speak with your new teacher."

Bonnie started trotting to keep up with her mother, who was already heading up the steep, twisting laneway leading to the bush. She started swinging her blue tin lunch pail for fun, but her clothes were making her more clumsy than usual. Her wool stockings were itchy, and the garters holding them up bit into her legs.

She had to admit that the rest of her clothes weren't too bad. Even though she didn't have much money, Mum always made sure Bonnie looked stylish. Today, she was wearing a navy blue pleated skirt that her mother had turned upside down and re-hemmed, so the thin parts could be at the very bottom. A clean, starched white middy blouse with a navy blue collar hid the worn bits at the top of her skirt.

"It's too bad this path goes right through the middle of the woods. Do be careful. I'm trying to get you to school on time and with no rips and tears in your clothes—at least for the first day."

"Golly, Mum. It's hard to walk in these new shiny shoes!" said Bonnie.

"Bite your tongue, child. I had to give up buying a new pair for myself to get those."

Bonnie noticed the holes in the sides of her mother's brown Oxfords. "I'm sorry. But could I take off my shoes and walk in my bare feet for a while? It'll save wear on them."

Mum huffed, "Keep them on! I will not let you go to school in bare feet."

Shadows fell across the path in the woods. Bonnie didn't mind trees, but there seemed to be too many right here.

"Do I have to go through these woods when I go to school by myself?" she asked.

"Yes, but you can see the trail easily. When you see more light come through the maple and oak trees, you'll know you're near the end of the woods."

They'd come to the edge of the woods and could see the rolling hills beside the Johnsons' farm.

They were on the road now, and Mum picked up the pace. "Now, Bonnie, before we get to school, I feel I should prepare you a little."

"Prepare me?"

"Yes. Sometimes, schoolchildren pick on the new kid."

"What do you mean?"

46

"Well, when my sister and I started a new school, the children would put our coats and toques on the floor. Viola would get to the cloakroom before me and pick them up. But eventually it got to her, and when she told me what had been going on, she started crying. Well, even though I'm two years younger than Viola, I wasted no time on tears, I can tell you!

"The next day I went around the whole room and dropped all the other coats and toques on the floor and hung mine and Viola's back up on their nails. Then I waited as the pupils came in one and two at a time to get their coats. I'd have fought them if they'd tried to take our coats down again."

"You...what...?"

"Yes. The ones that complained got a good yelling-at by me. You have to stand up for yourself in a new school. It's the only way or they'll take advantage."

Bonnie looked up at her strong, brave mother and felt fear rising in her throat. She wasn't a scrapper like her mother. For a while they walked on in silence. Bonnie hardly saw the dusty road beneath her feet, or the rail fence and thick bush on either side of the road. Her mind was now on unknown dangers ahead of her. They crossed a bridge over the gleaming blue waters of Indian River, and Bonnie looked around fearfully for the school building. The dozen or so houses they passed were mostly frame and clapboard—smaller than most farm homes—but there were two brick ones off the road to the right and behind trees. There was only one side street. It branched off to the south.

"Now, here's my advice to you," said Mum as they headed

47

past the last house in the village. "Stand up for yourself but don't go tattling to the teacher! No one likes a tattletale."

"But the teacher should know what—"

"He's too busy to know everything."

"He!" Bonnie gasped. "Mum...did you say *he*? Is it a man? I've never had a man teacher before!"

"Bonnie! Pull yourself together! I'm just trying to prepare you. Now, here's the school. Don't worry too much about being the new kid here. You'll do well, just like you always do with your lessons."

Mum opened a heavy wooden gate just underneath a flaming red maple tree and pointed across a field of goldenrod and asters. There stood the little, grey clapboard schoolhouse. But Bonnie was staring at the strange swing hanging from the tree. A long, heavy rope was tied to a thick branch high up in the tree. Near the bottom it divided, one part going into an inverted V with a seat across the widest part, the other hanging limply to the ground.

Bonnie followed her mother to the schoolhouse. As they came closer, she saw it had sagging, wooden steps up to the small stoop. An old shed stood at the side where wood was stacked and where pupils had once left horses and wagons. At the moment, however, there was no one in sight.

"Where is everyone, Mum?"

"They're all inside, working on their lessons."

"We're late!"

"No, I timed it this way. Now that the pupils are busy, the teacher will have time to meet us."

As they walked up the wooden steps, Bonnie looked right through the cracks and holes to the dusty ground below. But she did not see anything. She was thinking about her new teacher—a man.

They walked quietly through the small vestibule to the next door, where Mum knocked briskly.

In a minute, the door opened.

"Good morning, Mrs...." Bonnie jumped as the teacher stood there in front of them. He was slim, with grey-green eyes and reddish-brown hair. He looked younger than some of the boys at the back.

"I'm Mrs. Brown," said Mum. "We're new in the neighbourhood, Mr. McDougall. So I've come to enrol my daughter Bonnie in class today."

"And this is Bonnie?" the teacher asked.

"Yes, and here's a report from Miss Anderson, her teacher at the Massassaga school. That's in Prince Edward County. Bonnie attended that school for the past three years."

"Who's that? Shirley Temple?" a voice grumbled from the back of the room. "Do a dance for us, squirt."

Mr. McDougall lifted his head and gave the back-bench boys a look that would have made a giant shrink.

"I've heard you have a good, iron hand," said Mum.

"Yes, I do—when it's needed."

"I'll leave you to it, then," said Bonnie's mother, handing Mr. McDougall the report. Then she turned and disappeared out the door she had entered.

It all happened so quickly that Bonnie's "goodbye" didn't

have time to come out. It turned into a hiccup instead. She stood there, stunned, staring at the four-foot, black box-stove near the door. It had a tin frame around it, which Bonnie thought was strange. Her last school was heated from a big furnace in the basement.

Inside the schoolhouse, the October sun was shining through the tall, narrow windows, throwing beams of dust and light on rows and rows of wooden desks. As Mum had predicted, most of the twenty-five pupils were busy writing in their scribblers. Bonnie looked for Archie and Angela, but she was so nervous she could not even spot Archie's white-blond hair among the darker heads. In the back row, on the east side, sat five big boys who looked too old even for Grade Eight. One of those had called her a squirt.

"Come here, Bonnie," said Mr. McDougall, ignoring the second hiccup and motioning her to the front of the room. "Stand beside my desk and I'll introduce you to the class."

Bonnie's hiccups turned into hacking coughs. Mr. McDougall ignored them, too. He just sat down in the big armchair behind his desk and said, "Class, we have a new pupil, Bonnie Brown. I know you will make her welcome at recess. For now, please go back to your work. Lawrence and Tom—no recess for you this morning. You'll be staying in and cleaning the blackboards. Now, Bonnie," his voice became softer, "I have some questions to ask you."

"Yes, ss…irrr," said Bonnie, stopping a cough by putting her red polka-dot handkerchief over her mouth. As she walked closer to Mr. McDougall's desk, she noticed a head of white-blond hair out of the corner of her eye. Archie! So he was at school today. Maybe she'd find Angela in a minute, too.

"To begin with," said Mr. McDougall, "what grade did you start this September?"

"Grades Four and Five, sir," Bonnie coughed.

"How could you possibly be in two grades at the same time?"

"Well, I finished Grade Three last Easter; so the teacher started me in Grade Four. She said I'd be finished Grade Four by this Christmas, and could finish Grade Five by—"

"Enough! How many years have you gone to school?"

"Three."

"How old are you?"

"I turned nine at the end of August."

"You are the right age for Grade Four." Mr. McDougall took a book from the stack on his desk and handed it to Bonnie. "You'll do the same exercises as the Grade Fours. Turn to page ten in the arithmetic book and start with those sums." He pointed to his copy of the book on the front of his desk.

"But, sir, we used that very same book, and I did all those sums. I'm on page ninety-eight!"

"Do you have all those answers with you?"

"No, sir. Only the report from Miss Anderson." They had left Massassaga in such a hurry that all of Bonnie's scribblers were still at the school.

"I'll read the report in a while. For now, sit at the empty desk in the seat beside Betty."

Mr. McDougall gestured toward a pale-haired girl at

the front of the room, then rose and turned toward the blackboard. As Bonnie walked toward Betty's desk, someone on the other side of the classroom leaned out, grinning and waving—Archie. Bonnie smiled and waved back, relieved.

A tall, lanky boy got up from a back seat, hiked up his dark blue overalls, and slouched his way toward the pencil sharpener at the window. A small scuffle took place as he passed Archie's desk. Archie was left sitting on the floor.

"Yowww!" said Archie, glaring after the back of the boy.

Every eye turned. Loud guffaws came from the back.

"Take your seat, Bonnie," Mr. McDougall said sharply. "You've interrupted us enough for one day. Back to work, everyone!"

Archie slid back into his seat, his face flaming red with shame.

Bonnie sat down beside Betty, a pale girl who peered at Bonnie through round, steel-rimmed glasses. Then Betty pushed her scribbler toward her new classmate. "You may copy my answers," she whispered.

Bonnie looked at the page. It was a mess of blurred numbers and erased sums. There were even two holes where Betty had erased too many times. The one or two answers that Bonnie could read were wrong.

"No, thank you!" said Bonnie.

Betty snatched back her workbook in disgust.

Bonnie opened her own scribbler and started copying out the questions from the textbook, as Miss Anderson had taught her to do.

As she was copying, Mr. McDougall came pacing by. "What are you doing?" he said, peering at Bonnie's work. "Just filling time, I see—you haven't added up a single sum. I doubt you are ready for Grade Four, never mind Grade Five!"

"But, sir, I'll answer them. This is the way we did it back home."

"A likely story," Mr. McDougall sniffed. "Now, stop copying the questions and start writing down the answers."

Bonnie knew she had better do as she was told. Mr. McDougall had that teacher tone of voice that meant trouble could be on the way. She started writing down the answers, and in a few minutes she had finished the whole exercise.

"Grade Four, bring all your arithmetic answers to the front," said Mr. McDougall a few minutes later.

The Grade Fours scrambled forward and left their scribblers in a pile on his desk. Mr. McDougall straightened up the pile and then ignored the books.

"Now, class," he announced, "it's recess time. All but the five of you at the back are dismissed."

Most of the pupils jumped up and rushed for the door in a mass. Only the big boys stayed in their seats—and Bonnie. She'd noticed a copy of *Anne of Green Gables* on a bookshelf against the wall. Grandma Brown had told her about that book. Ever since, she'd wanted to read it.

"What are you waiting for? Go out and play," Mr. McDougall told her. His grey-green eyes made her think of a garter snake.

Bonnie got up slowly and marched down the long aisle between the empty rows of desks. She opened the door at the back and stepped out into the sunshine. There on the steps stood her new neighbours—a smiling Angela, a giggling Marianne Hubbs, and Archie. He grinned at Bonnie and said, "Guess what I found under the steps!"

Once she got over the sight of yet another snake, Bonnie had a fine time playing hopscotch with her new girlfriends. When Mr. McDougall rang the bell, Angela went to the Grade Six section and Bonnie went back to sit with the Grade Fours. Angela had also skipped a grade. That gave Bonnie hope that Mr. McDougall might change his mind.

Not yet, though. The Grade Four scribblers were handed out again, and Bonnie was left to sit in front of the sums she'd finished before recess, doing nothing. Meanwhile, her new teacher was telling the Grade Fives all about the French explorer, Jacques Cartier.

"And so he arrived at Hochelaga," Mr. McDougall said. "Now, what do we call Hochelaga today?" The Grade Five pupils were looking down, hoping Mr. McDougall wouldn't ask them to answer. Bonnie couldn't resist the impulse to rescue them.

"Bonnie, why is your hand waving in the air?"

"It's now the city of Montréal!"

"Young lady, I am teaching Grade Five. You are in Grade Four. Do not interrupt. Continue with your own work."

"But, sir, I've finished."

"My name is Mr. McDougall! Address me as such. And check over your answers. You could not possibly have answered them all correctly in such a short time!"

Bonnie looked down at her scribbler. She knew all the answers were right. But she blinked and said, "Yes, Mr. McDougall."

No teacher had ever spoken to Bonnie in that tone of voice. In fact, Miss Anderson thought it was wonderful that Bonnie listened in on the lessons ahead of her grade.

Miss Anderson! Bonnie looked over at her new teacher. The report from Miss Anderson was still sticking out the top of his back pocket. When he read it, Mr. McDougall would know that Bonnie really was ready for Grade Five. She was sure of it.

She would just have to be patient and wait till after class to find out.

* * * *

Finally, at the end of a long first day (filled with more lessons that Miss Anderson had already taught Bonnie), Mr. McDougall stood up to address the class.

"Everyone, close your books," he said. "You may take your scribblers home, but leave all textbooks in your desks. If you wish to copy out questions to answer at home, you may stay to do that now." A ripple of laughter ran across the back of the room where the big boys sat.

"Dismissed!" Mr. McDougall snapped. The bigger boys stampeded for the door and the others followed. Only two pupils remained—Lizzie Johnson, who was in Grade Eight and studying for her high school entrance exams in June, and Bonnie.

"Bonnie Brown, come to the front," Mr. McDougall snapped again.

"Yes, sir."

"Bonnie," he said severely, "this report from your teacher is simply last June's report card—that is all!"

"But, sir, I thought—"

"What is my name?"

"Mr. McDougall. I thought—"

"Your report card states that you completed Grade Three successfully last year, and achieved fine grades doing so. But without some evidence of Grade Four work completed, I cannot promote you beyond your proper grade. You will continue with Grade Four, but there will be no nonsense about completing Grade Five this school year as well. Do you understand?"

Bonnie blinked again. She could see there was nothing she could do.

"Thank you, Mr. McDougall," she said politely. Then, for the second time that day, she marched alone down the long aisle between the desks.

SIX: TROUBLE AND TURNIPS

Archie was waiting for her just outside the door. "Don't worry, Bonnie, no snakes!" He beamed, his freckles bunching up on his nose. He had found another aspen branch and was waving it in the air. But Bonnie could not see him too well. She was blinking to keep back the tears.

Then a hand took hold of her own smaller one. "C'mon, Bonnie." Angela smiled. "We're going home by the long way round. That way we'll go right by your woods!"

Archie was as nice as could be all the way home, and Angela picked a wildflower bouquet for Bonnie to take to her mother. "Don't worry about Mr. McDougall," Angela told Bonnie. "He's just not used to letting people do two grades in one year. It was the last teacher who let me skip a grade. Most teachers just take it for granted that we can skip grades. But he's new at the job."

Bonnie appreciated the thought, but still, she breathed a sigh of relief when Angela and Archie turned along the north-south road toward their home. She just wanted to be alone.

A flock of geese flew in a V over Bonnie's head as she turned into the path that went through the woods. It seemed Bonnie and her Mum and Dad were the only ones in the neighbourhood who did not have a proper place to live. She supposed that everyone else owned their farms but theirs was rented. And it was far away from everyone. At least the Hubbs lived just south of the Johnsons. And back in Massassaga, the farmhouses were all in a row along the highway at the front of the farms. They weren't stuck in the middle of the land where no one could see them. Here, their house was the most remote—you had to pass through woods and hills and hills to reach it.

Bonnie threw herself down on a pile of red maple and brown oak leaves. Her blue lunch pail rolled out of her hand and down the hilly path. Her bouquet of goldenrod and asters dropped to the ground beside her. She stared up at the sky, but a stately pine tree blocked her view. It seemed to be observing everything—the chipmunks and squirrels hustling about and the breezes ruffling the leaves at the tops of the other trees. The pine just stood there silent and serene while here on the forest floor, small creatures scurried about in lively activity.

A short time later, Bonnie gathered up her things with a sigh, and walked on.

"What kept you, Bonnie?" Dad asked when Bonnie reached the bottom of the long lane and unhooked the gate to the barnyard.

"I…I…it's a long walk home from school!" Bonnie stuttered.

"And a long way back for the cows, too!"

"Oh, Dad. I forgot all about the cows! I'm sorry! I'll go back for them right away."

Dad took his watch out of the pocket in the bib of his overalls. "Well, you could, but now that you're here, you might as well get yourself a piece of bread and brown sugar before you head back out to the pasture."

While she was grateful for the break, Bonnie didn't tell

her father that she no longer liked plain bread topped with a sprinkle of brown sugar. She wished she could have fried donuts and oatmeal cookies like other kids had.

"Cheer up, Bonnie!" her father was saying. "Boots will help you round up the cows. He's a spirited little fellow." Hitching up his overalls a notch, Dad walked back to the barn.

Bonnie nodded and headed for the house. She looked down at the bouquet she was still clutching in her hand. Mum liked flowers but she wouldn't want these. Bonnie threw them on the ground before she opened the gate into the dooryard.

She was not surprised to find her mother still cleaning. Bonnie watched as Mum tipped boiling water from the big copper boiler on the stove into the mop-pail. She shook the soft-soap carrier into it, then dashed the mop back and forth till suds started to rise up over the edge of the pail.

"Bonnie!" Mum exclaimed disapprovingly.

"What?"

"You're a mess! Your skirt is all wrinkled and your white middy is filthy. What happened?"

Bonnie looked down. It was true. Her middy was covered with huge streaks of dirt from the leaf-pile in the woods. Her navy blue skirt was wrinkled and dirty, too.

"Go and change immediately. I'll have to wash your clothes right away to have them ready for tomorrow," Mum said. "And put your lunch pail by the sink to be washed with the supper dishes."

"Yes, Mum."

Bonnie ran up the steep back stairs to the only place she

MILFORD PUBLIC LIBRARY
330 FAMILY DRIVE
MILFORD, MI 48381

could really call hers. It wasn't a bedroom, exactly. Mum and Dad had put her bed on the stair landing close to the stovepipe, so that she would keep warm in winter. At least, that was what they told her. Bonnie thought her parents wanted her next to their room so they could keep an eye on her. She was always trying to read in bed and forgetting to blow out the coal-oil lamp.

Bonnie stepped out of her skirt and tried to pull the middy up over her head. But it got stuck because she'd forgotten to unbutton the front V-piece. Maybe she really was the clumsiest child in Ontario. That's what her mother always said. Or maybe the problem was the clothes. She had no trouble slipping on her faded red shirt and stepping into her homemade blue patched overalls.

The kitchen was neat and quiet when Bonnie came downstairs. Mum's stiffly starched red gingham curtains were hanging beside the windows, and the long, bumpy couch at the north side of the room was covered with soft, red feather-pillows. The sewing machine, Mum's pride and joy, was in front of the back window, and her dark buffet was standing against the east wall. The stove stood in front of the opposite wall, its gleaming black top polished to a shine, as usual. Mum sure knew how to make a house look good.

As Bonnie walked past the stove on her way to the pantry, she lifted the lid of the big frying pan at the back. She took a sniff and nearly gagged. Then she peeked inside. The pan was filled with horrible turnip chunks. Warmed-up turnip chunks. Fresh ones were bad enough—but warmed up! That was too terrible to think about.

Bonnie felt so sickened by the smell that she didn't even bother going into the pantry for a snack of bread and butter. She went right outside and headed for the barnyard. Boots came bounding up beside her and they trotted off to the pasture.

"Go get 'em! Round 'em up!" said Bonnie when they arrived at the last steep field.

Boots went off in a streak of gold and rounded up all four of the black-and-white Holsteins in no time at all.

"Atta boy, Boots! Atta boy!"

Boots raced back to Bonnie, his tail wagging. He circled around her like a spinning top. Bonnie reached out to pat his thick coat. At least Boots was one good thing that had happened in this strange place.

But Boots did not stop to be patted. He rushed past Bonnie and started barking at the cows. The four Holsteins broke into a run, their heavy udders swaying from side to side. Bonnie knew that meant trouble. It was not good for cows with full udders to run like that; they would be harder to milk when they were all excited.

"C'mon back, Boots! Here, Boots! C'mere, you bad boy!" The dog didn't seem to hear. He was too happy thinking he'd been successful. Bonnie kept running and running and calling out to the pup. Finally, she caught up to him and grabbed him by the scruff of his neck.

"Stop! Stop!" she shouted. Boots finally understood. He dropped his fluffy tail and put it between his legs.

Still, Boots had perked up again by the time Bonnie had the cows at the barnyard gate.

"Good job, Bonnie," said Dad. "You did just fine!"

Bonnie thought she'd better explain what Boots had done, in case Dad had trouble milking. Dad frowned at what she told him. She knew how much he valued his prize cows.

"I'd better train him a little more this week, then. But don't get too used to the holiday," he cautioned. "Next week you'll have your job back."

* * * *

"Eat up, Bonnie. You're too thin. You need all the strength you can get."

"Sorry, Mum, I'm just not hungry anymore!" Bonnie looked down at the blob of mashed turnips and the fried fish patty on her plate.

"It doesn't matter whether you're hungry or not. You need to eat."

"Please, Mum, couldn't we have something else besides suckerballs and turnips? Maybe an orange once in a while?"

The minute she said the word "orange," Bonnie knew it was a mistake.

"Oranges are very expensive," said Dad. "We simply cannot afford them."

"And why can't we afford them, Thomas? Because you expanded your farm too quickly down in Massassaga. You shouldn't have bought the best prize Holstein cows. Dad's

62

Jerseys give just as much milk and more cream! We wouldn't be stuck in this place if you'd been reasonable."

"How was I to know the Depression would hit, Amelia? Lots of people are in worse shape than we are."

So Dad was calling Mum by her proper name. He did that when he was angry. Bonnie knew she mustn't say anything or both her parents would yell at her. She wished she didn't have to hear all this again.

"And those old folks you borrowed money from? They don't need to be paid back so quickly!"

"If you were elderly, you wouldn't say that!"

"They're not pushing you, Thomas. It's your pride. Of course, you must repay them. But do it more slowly! Have *they* complained?"

That was a good question. Bonnie stared up at her father, but he looked right through her as though she didn't exist.

"No. But it's my duty to pay them back as soon as I can. They're old and they'll be worrying. And we're not starving!"

"Well, not yet, Thomas, but wait till winter comes! What if some of that fish goes bad? Or the turnips get too mouldy?"

"We have lots of fish," said Dad. "And you're a clever cook, Amy."

Good! thought Bonnie. He was calling her Amy again! Things were going to calm down now. That sick feeling in Bonnie's stomach was starting to feel a little better.

"You can think of a million ways to make things tasty. This fry-up is just excellent, by the way." Dad didn't like fighting any more than Bonnie did.

Bonnie stared at her plate, lifted her fork, and started to eat. One mouthful at a time, she would get it down. And she would never mention an *orange* again. When they saw her eating, maybe they'd stop this fighting.

"Well, thank you," said Mum, "but no one wants to eat the same fish a million different ways! When I was a girl, we worked hard, but we always had good meals. That was because Dad hunted. When we ran out of meat, he took his gun and shot a deer or a rabbit or—"

Dad's face went pale. "Amy…Amy…please don't talk about hunting. I cannot stand the sight of blood! You know that!"

"Yes, but I don't understand it. You could get used to it, but instead you'd rather putter around on the farm all day."

"Putter? I wouldn't call ploughing up those tough old fields *puttering*. I wouldn't call milking and mucking out horse and cow stables *puttering*! I'm working just as hard as any man can."

"Well, so am I." Her voice was louder now.

"I never said you didn't," mumbled Dad.

Mum was not consoled. "I get up at the same time as you every morning, and every night you're snoring before I even get to bed. I work longer hours than you do!"

"I know, Amy." Dad's voice was much quieter now, and he looked sorry. Mum was going to win the argument again, thought Bonnie with a sigh. She usually did, whether she was right or wrong. Most of their arguments started with talk of the debt.

One thing was for sure, Bonnie decided. When she grew

64

up, she would never buy anything she couldn't pay for right then. She would never, *ever* be in debt!

SEVEN: TOM AND SLINKY

"Get down here, Bonnie!" Mum yelled from the bottom of the stairs.

"I'm dressing!"

"Well, hurry up about it!"

Mum had hung Bonnie's white middy and navy skirt on the bedside washstand made out of an old orange crate that Mum had found in the trash behind a Belleville store. The clothes were all cleaned and ironed, just like a miracle.

Bonnie whipped them off the stand, put them on, and hurried down the stairs. The minute Mum saw her daughter, she rushed over with a big apron made out of a flour bag. That would protect Bonnie's top from all the porridge she would soon be spilling. But this time Bonnie downed her porridge at lightning speed without a single mistake.

Two minutes later, her mother was whisking Bonnie out the door with her blue tin lunch pail, her scribbler, and a warm navy jacket. "Off you go, and pay attention to your teacher. You're a smart girl, but he's smarter. So listen to what he says."

"That reminds me, Mum," Bonnie began, "Mr. McDougall only has my June report card. Didn't Miss Anderson give us anything else? Anything about my Grade Five work?"

"What do you mean, Bonnie? I gave Mr. McDougall all we had—your June report card. We left suddenly. Don't you remember? We did not have time to pick up anything else— not even your school books!"

Bonnie had suspected this but wanted to be sure, just in case some other sort of evidence could still be found. Now there was no hope whatsoever.

Out in the barnyard, Boots was racing around Duke and Rose. Dad was hitching them up to the plough. He shouted, "Have a good day, Bonnie. Work hard!"

"Oh, sure," said Bonnie. How could she have a good day doing work she had already done last spring? What was the point in working hard? Bonnie slowed her pace, a feeling of gloom and dread creeping over her. Why hurry to that school?

Dad didn't notice. He went merrily on his way as he whistled a cheery tune.

* * * *

"Hey, Bonnie! Come over here and play on our team!" Archie yelled from the other side of the schoolhouse gate. The grassy area between the asters and the school was wet with dew, but no one seemed to mind. Two teams were already lining up to play.

Oh, no, thought Bonnie. *Baseball!*

She started thinking up excuses. Mum wouldn't want her to get her shoes wet. She also wouldn't want her to get dirt on her skirt and middy. Maybe...Bonnie stopped herself. If she used excuses like that, she knew the other students would make fun of her forever. So she just smiled and said, "Not this morning. I have reading to do!"

That was not really a lie, for she hadn't forgotten *Anne of*

Green Gables. There was a chance Mr. McDougall would let her read it before classes began.

"Why ask that darn snippet anyway?" one of the boys jeered as Bonnie walked up the steps to the school. "I'll bet she can't throw or catch—let alone hit a ball!"

Bonnie turned her head away and marched into the school.

Inside, the room was empty and quiet. Mr. McDougall was busy marking papers at his desk; so Bonnie tiptoed to her seat, not wanting to disturb him. She stashed her scribbler in the desk, then leaned over. She could almost reach the bookshelf. If she moved another inch toward the edge of her seat, she wouldn't have to walk across the creaking floor boards to fetch the book.

Another half-inch...another...

Crash! Bonnie fell to the floor, and a few novels fell down around her shoulders.

"Bonnie Brown! What in heaven's name are you doing?"

Bonnie stood up and dusted off her skirt. A book with a worn-out cover dropped from her lap. "I'm sorry, sir...Sir McDougall, I mean Mr. Sir, I was just trying to—"

"It's 'Mr. McDougall,' Bonnie. Now, have you signed that book out or did you imagine that you could simply take whatever you pleased?"

"No, I didn't know, Mr. McDougall...it's just...I didn't want to play baseball in the schoolyard...and..."

"And you think that gives you special permission to come in and take books?"

"No, sir, I mean Mr. McDougall, I didn't want to interrupt

your work to ask for a book—"

"Well, Bonnie, I know it's difficult coming to a new school, but you have to make an effort to learn new rules. In the future, be sure to sign out each book before you take it. See that pencil and paper above the shelf? If you sign the book out first, you don't have to ask permission. For now, though, just put those books back on the shelf and sit back at your desk. It's nearly nine o'clock and everyone will be coming in soon."

Bonnie spent the rest of the morning trying to make sure Mr. McDougall didn't notice her. From time to time, she could not resist stealing a glance at the bookshelf. The words *Anne of Green Gables* were still glowing there in large gold letters, on the spine of the book.

When the wall clock at the back of the room showed twelve, Bonnie breathed a sigh of relief. Lunchtime! She'd have a whole hour away from Mr. McDougall's eagle eyes, and Angela would be waiting for her outside the door. They'd have a nice walk through the nearby fields while everyone else played baseball.

Bonnie left her seat with the others and walked into the girls' cloakroom. Her dark blue jacket was hanging on its hook and her lunch pail was on the shelf above it. She picked up her lunch pail and raced out to the schoolyard where a gentle breeze tossed a few leaves over the ground.

Under the maple tree, a couple of the big boys were tussling over a baseball bat. But Angela and Archie were nowhere in sight. Nor was Mr. McDougall. He had gone for his lunch hour to his boarding house, which was at the other end of the hamlet.

"What are you having for lunch?" Marianne bounded up beside Bonnie and slapped her across the shoulders.

"Oh...I was just looking for Angela and Archie and..." Bonnie said. "And here you are!"

"Weren't you looking for me, too?"

"Oh, yes, yes! But where is everyone else?"

"They went home for lunch. They often do that when the weather's good."

"Oh..." Bonnie tried not to look disappointed.

"So don't you want to have lunch with me?" Marianne's wispy, blonde braids flew sideways as she turned away.

Bonnie grabbed Marianne's shoulder and said, "Of course, I do!" Marianne was a bit bouncy, but she was friendly.

"Do most kids go home for lunch?" Bonnie asked as they squeezed between the other children on the steps of the school.

"Sure do! Till it snows."

Bonnie's desk mate, Betty, inched over toward the two girls. "I usually go home for lunch too," she said, "but my parents went to Peterborough today." She took a huge orange out of her paper lunch bag and started to peel it.

An orange! How could Betty's parents afford to buy her an orange—for her school lunch? Bonnie couldn't help watching as Betty popped a piece into her mouth—then another, and another.

"Would you like a piece?" Betty asked at last.

70

Bonnie smiled. She could hardly believe her luck. "Yes, please!" she exclaimed.

Betty handed a section to Bonnie and held out another piece for Marianne.

"No, thank you," Marianne said in a cold tone. Betty looked hurt. She got up and walked inside the school.

"This orange is good," said Bonnie. "Why didn't you want any?"

"Because Betty always wants payment. She'll expect you to give her answers for arithmetic this afternoon. If you don't, she'll never offer you another piece."

"Are her parents rich?"

"No! They're poor, but they're on Relief. Most of the people in Lang are on Relief. In Peterborough, people can go to soup kitchens, but not here. So some people accept money from the government."

"Oh," said Bonnie. Relief didn't sound too bad. She wondered why her own parents were so against it.

As if answering her question, Marianne said, "We farmers never take Relief. We're a step above that."

"What is Relief, exactly?"

"It's like charity from the government, to keep poor people from starving. Most folks won't accept it."

"Well, the people in Lang don't have farm food the way we do. They don't have cows to milk. So I guess they really need Relief."

"That's true," Marianne said and thought for a while. "Well, anyway, I hate it that they can eat oranges and bananas and

71

other things, too, and we can't!"

The two girls stared down at their toes as a dark cloud sent a big shadow across the schoolyard.

"Maybe we'll be rich someday!" Marianne said brightly. "I'd like to be a nurse. I'm always taking care of sick animals."

"So why don't you be a vet?"

"I'd like that, but did you ever know of a girl vet?"

Bonnie thought. "No, but there are women doctors—so there must be some women vets, too."

"I never knew a woman doctor."

"Well, our doctor at Belleville was a woman—Dr. Connor. And she was the best doctor in the whole countryside. She travelled around in her horse and buggy, visiting patients. It was five miles across that cold Bay Bridge from Belleville just to our place!"

"I still think I might like to be a nurse," said Marianne.

Then, as the shadow of another cloud crossed the yard, Bonnie sensed someone standing in front of them. It was Lawrence, whom all the kids called Slinky, and another big boy—probably Tom, Bonnie thought. Slinky was smiling with his mouth open wide, a huge, greasy grin that matched the greasy light brown hair that straggled over his ears. He was wearing a grey undershirt under his coveralls, and mud was smeared under his left eye. His small green eyes squinted at Bonnie.

"Lunch hour's only half over, Tom," said Marianne. "Are you looking for your sister Pearl?"

"Nope. She's still at home. I ate fast and came back early."

Tom was a sturdy boy with broad shoulders. He brushed a shock of dark brown hair off his forehead and stared at Bonnie with large, cold, blue eyes. He was not smiling.

But his friend Slinky laughed a big, ugly laugh. "Do you know who's sitting next to you?" he drawled.

"Of course I do. Bonnie Brown, our new neighbour."

"Aren't you afraid to sit beside her?"

"Why should I be?"

"She comes from the consumption house. My parents say she shouldn'a bin allowed to come to school and infect us all. They went to the health-medic in Keene, but Dr. Wright says there ain't nothin' he kin do 'bout it."

"Yeah, so we figger we will," Tom sneered.

"Bonnie, go run to the girls' toilet," Marianne whispered. "They won't dare follow you there!" Then Marianne stood up and looked—first Tom, then Slinky—right in the eye. "Mind your own business or I'll tell the teacher." Marianne pushed Slinky's chest with the flat of her hand.

I will not run away, Bonnie told herself, standing her ground. *I won't let the bullies see I'm scared. Mum said to stand my ground!* But she felt her heart thumping.

In the next second, Bonnie felt four rough hands grab her by the shoulders. Marianne pulled back on her middy collar, but the boys won out. Pupils all over the schoolyard were now staring as Tom and Slinky pulled Bonnie across the lawn.

Bonnie's heart was pounding harder and harder. She started screaming, "Let me go! Let—me—go!"

But the boys kept dragging her across the grass.

Was no one going to help her?

Now the bullies were throwing Bonnie onto the cement platform of the school water pump. Tom was working the pump handle, and Slinky hung on to her arms so tightly she could not move.

Maybe they were just going to make her drink some cold water. She stopped struggling and watched.

Then, in a sudden movement, Slinky tipped her head under the spout and yelled, "Keep pumping, Tom! We'll get rid of them darn germs!"

Now, Bonnie squirmed desperately to be free. Then she heard something else. It was…it was cheering. All the kids were egging the bullies on! But why? Did they hate her? Did they think she was a show-off because she answered a Grade Five question in class? Or a snob because she wouldn't play baseball?

"Hold 'er head under! Don't want water all over that purty dress. McDougall would tan us for sure. But let me at that ugly mop of hair. Probably full of germs—and cooties!"

Bonnie gasped for air, but Tom kept on pumping. The water got colder and colder. There was water in Bonnie's eyes, her nose, her mouth, and her ears.

She was sputtering and coughing, but the water kept coming.

"See, what did I tell ya? Consumption! Ain't she fulla germs? Better wash 'er up some more!"

"Stop, you deadbeats!" cried Marianne. "Do you want to hang for murder? She could choke to death."

"Watch your language, Miss Prissy, or I'll tell your Dad,"

said Tom.

"Mr. McDougall will be back soon!" yelled Marianne.

Finally, Tom stopped pumping and Slinky threw Bonnie on the grass. When she could open her eyes again, she saw a whole group of kids—maybe half the school—walking away with their backs turned.

Only one person stood beside Bonnie.

"Here," said a voice. It was Marianne's. She wiped Bonnie's face with a white, lace-trimmed handkerchief. "I know a nice sunny stone behind the school. We can sit there till you dry out."

Blinking back her tears, Bonnie let Marianne lead her around to the other side of the school. In the distance she heard more sounds of cheering. It was the same kids, but they were playing baseball now.

"You just wait, Bonnie, till I tell Mr. McDougall," said Marianne. "I bet he'll keep them in after school for a month. You'll see!"

"Oh, no! Marianne," exclaimed Bonnie. "You can't tell on them! It would only make matters worse. Anyway, I don't want to be a tattletale!"

"Well, you wouldn't be if *I* tattle, and *I* won't mind what they think." Marianne was still very angry.

Bonnie grabbed her friend's hand and pleaded. "You can't. Please, for me—don't do it! Mum says I have to stand up for myself. You have to let it go, Marianne."

For a long minute, Marianne stared at Bonnie's pleading eyes, and then she nodded.

* * * *

On the way home from school, Bonnie followed Archie along the path in the woods.

"All the kids at school hate me. You went home at noon. And Slinky and Tom drenched my head under the pump. The rest of the kids cheered—except for Marianne."

"I heard. Awful sorry, Bonnie. But you're okay now, aren't you?"

"Yes, but—"

"They don't hate you. It's just that you're the new kid. Look, I'm taking my lunch tomorrow. So you'll be okay. Now, stop thinking about those boys. I want you to meet my crow."

"Oh Archie, I don't think—"

"Quiet, Bonnie! You could scare the crow away!"

"Then how do I tell you when I want to say something?"

"That's what the aspen branches are for, remember? You tap me on the shoulder with a branch. When I turn around, you whisper what you want to say. Now, what did you want to say?"

"Oh, never mind," said Bonnie. But after a while she tapped him with her branch.

"Yes?" Archie whispered.

"Are you sure about this crow, Archie?"

"Of course I am. I told you—it came to me once. Just wait. You'll see it one of these days."

"Well, I'm tired of tramping through the woods. Let's get

home so you can have a good visit with Boots."

As soon as they were out of the woods, Archie cried, "Race ya!" and ran down the hill toward the barnyard.

Bonnie let him go. Though he hadn't said so, she knew that Archie had walked home with her to make sure the bullies didn't follow. She was grateful, but now she had to think by herself. Should she tell her parents what had happened?

Bonnie decided not to say anything. What was the use? Mum would just say she should stand up to the bullies. After all, that's what Mum had done. Bonnie hated to admit it, but she knew she wasn't nearly as brave as Mum.

"Wait for me, Archie!" she yelled, grabbing the top of the barnyard gate and jumping over it. "Wow, Archie! Look what I did! I cleared the gate in just one leap!"

But Archie wasn't listening. He was running ahead with Boots at his heels. So Bonnie went chasing after the two of them. Soon they were all zigzagging around the barnyard.

EIGHT: SWING HIGH

Bonnie was in a complete daze as she walked to school one brisk Monday morning in early November. The afternoon before, Mrs. Elmhirst and her son, Roy, had visited the farm. Her parents had been pleased by the owner's compliments on their upkeep of the place.

Then Mrs. Elmhirst had asked Bonnie if she liked her new school.

"No," Bonnie had said, "I don't."

Bonnie could still see the hard stares from Mum and Dad. So she had added, "I do like school, but I don't like..."

Then, Roy the business man came to the rescue. He smiled and winked at her as he said, "Perhaps, you mean that you don't like being the new pupil." Bonnie had nodded and smiled with relief.

The visit over, her parents walked with the Elmhirsts to their Ford Lincoln. Roy turned to Dad and said, "Do you mind if I give something to Bonnie to help her in the new school?"

"It's fine with me," Dad said, smiling.

Roy turned around and pressed something into Bonnie's hand. She mumbled, "Thank you," in a very low voice. Mum did not like her accepting anything from anyone.

After their guests had gone, Bonnie ran upstairs to her bed and opened her hand. She could not believe her eyes. It was a whole quarter! Was she seeing things? Was it really that much? Yes, it was a quarter. She'd only ever had a nickel to spend. This was worth five of them!

She was still daydreaming about it the next morning, all the way to school. A nickel would buy a package of five suckers—big, round suckers all wrapped together in cellophane. She liked the orange and lemon best, but brown ones were good, too. Black was also nice, and even green candy wasn't too bad. But for a quarter, she could also buy a huge chocolate bar, or a big ice-cream cone with two rounded scoops side by side; or she could buy a delicious bottle of Orange Crush that would tickle all the way down her throat. But she finally decided to share it with her best friends—she would take them to the store at lunchtime.

The morning stretched out uneventfully. At noon, Bonnie, Marianne, and Angela stepped quickly along the pathway by the road that led to the general store. A brisk wind nipped at the girls' scarves and whipped them across their faces.

"Brrr! It's cold for this time of year," said Bonnie. In Massassaga, the days were usually sunny and snowless until December.

"Around here, once November comes, one can expect snow anytime," said Angela.

"And it probably won't leave till spring," said Marianne with a sigh.

As Marianne flung open the door of the little all-purpose store, the girls felt the rush of warm air from the pot-belly stove in the centre of the room. There was no one sitting in the chairs around the stove. Most folks were too busy now preparing their homes for winter.

"And what can I do for you fine ladies this afternoon?" asked Mr. Weir, the owner. He leaned against the shelves behind the counter and put his thumbs behind his suspenders.

"I am treating my friends today," Bonnie said proudly. "Can you show us your assortment of suckers?" Bonnie thought "assortment" was the right word. She liked the way it sounded, anyway.

Mr. Weir smiled broadly under his grey moustache as he limped around the counter. He had never recovered from an old war wound. "Here you are, ladies. Take a look at that jar! I have suckers in every colour of the rainbow. Five cents for five. But you must pick all different colours when purchasing from this jar—that is, for the price I said."

Bonnie and Marianne opened their eyes wide and let their jaws drop. Angela just smiled. Then all three circled around the jar like bees around a honeycomb. They chose red for Marianne, purple for Angela, and orange for Bonnie. That left only yellow and green for the last two.

"Goodbye, Mr. Weir." Bonnie waved as the three girls strutted out the door, candy in hand.

On the way back to school, the girls went past Betty's house, just as Betty was rushing out the door.

"Here," Bonnie shouted. "Have a sucker!" Betty gawked at Bonnie for a second, then quickly chose the yellow one.

There, thought Bonnie with satisfaction. She had paid for Betty's piece of orange. Too bad Betty had chosen the yellow sucker, though. Green tasted a little like soap. She hoped Archie wouldn't mind.

* * * *

The clock at the back of the room was ticking its way to two-thirty.

Bonnie was bored. She was still doing work she'd already completed the year before. She shoved her scribbler to the top of her desk and fished around in the pocket of her skirt. *Good!* she thought. The candy was safe inside its crinkly cellophane wrapper. She'd give it to Archie right after school. He'd be so surprised!

Bonnie looked back to the clock to see if it was three o'clock yet. No such luck. The minute hand had moved to two-thirty-two. As she was turning back to face the front of the room, she thought she saw a dark leaf sticking to the east window. But it wasn't a leaf. It was something with wings.

What could that be? Bonnie squinted hard at the big black thing. It was…no, it couldn't be…but, yes, it was…

A crow!

"Sir!" Bonnie cried out before she could stop herself.

"Bonnie Brown, are you the teacher today? The teacher is the only one who talks in class without being asked."

"But…but…"

"Well, out with it. What's the matter now?"

"There's a crow in the window, Sir McDougall…sir…Mr. McDougall!"

The whole class turned swiftly to the window with their eyes peering almost out of their heads.

Mr. McDougall strode to the window. The crow lifted first its left wing, then its right. Mr. McDougall raised his right eyebrow as if he was imitating it. Then the crow put its wings down and Mr. McDougall pushed his eyebrows together. The crow and the teacher stared at each other for a good half-minute.

"Well…!" Mr. McDougall said finally. "Class, put aside the work you are doing. I do believe we have the perfect opportunity for a science lesson." Groans came from the back of the classroom, but Mr. McDougall ignored them. "Crows are strong birds that prey on smaller creatures—like mice or doves, but very occasionally, they can become pets of humans—just like parrots. I have even heard that sometimes…"

As Mr. McDougall droned on, Bonnie looked at Archie. He waved back and nodded his head. While she had his attention, Bonnie thought she'd show him the sucker. She reached inside her skirt pocket and drew out the candy. Mr. McDougall had left the window and was about to write something on the board. She waved the sucker in the air.

With his eyes on the sucker, Archie waved back.

But Bonnie had misjudged her teacher's focus of attention.

"Bonnie!" Mr. McDougall exclaimed. "Whatever are you doing?"

Every eye now turned from the crow to Bonnie. The afternoon was turning out to be quite interesting!

"March right up here and put *that* on my desk," Mr. McDougall said sternly. "There is no eating during class hours. That includes no candy and no chewing gum. Didn't they teach you anything at that other school?"

Bonnie walked up to the desk and, with great sadness, set the candy down in front of Mr. McDougall—right beside the big leather strap.

"And, Bonnie, you will stay after school for your punishment. Archie, you too will stay."

Bonnie slinked back to her seat, her cheeks burning. Was she now going to get the strap? And with Archie watching? She shivered a little as she sat down. Then she noticed Betty looking at her with kind eyes. Maybe Betty wasn't so bad after all. And next time, Bonnie decided, she'd be more careful. After all, she still had four nickels tucked away in her pocket. She'd treat Archie yet.

Meanwhile, the crow had swooped away from the window. The afternoon's entertainment was over, and all returned to their lessons.

* * * *

"It's four o'clock. Close your books now, class," Mr. McDougall said, strolling down the centre aisle. Bonnie saw that the green sucker was still up at the front, right where she'd put it. At least the hateful teacher had not eaten it while the students were doing their desk work.

"Now, class dismissed!" Mr. McDougall snapped. "All except Bonnie and Archie. You...come to the front!" The teacher then looked down at something on his desk.

Standing at the front beside Archie, Bonnie's eyes were

fixed on the strap. It looked just like a piece of horse harness! How many lashes would she get? She had never been strapped at school before! She took a deep breath and tightened her hands into fists as she stood waiting.

Mr. McDougall looked up then and said, "Bonnie, you will write on the blackboard, 'I shall not play with candy in class.' I guess that fifty times will be enough. And Archie, you were waving for that candy when you should have been paying attention. So you can do the same. Now clean the boards and then start your writing."

Before long, Archie and Bonnie had erased the lessons, each picked up a piece of chalk, and started writing their lines at opposite ends of the blackboard: *I shall not play with candy in class*. After Bonnie had written the sentence five times, her vision started to blur. She shook her blonde curls and started in on line six. By line eight, the words started looking like nonsense. *I shall...Shall?* Who made up that word? It didn't mean anything, really!

Bonnie looked over at Archie. He was only at line five. Bonnie slowed down a bit so they'd finish at the same time. By line twenty, Bonnie was covered in chalk dust. It was in her throat and all over her navy skirt. By line twenty-five, she was coughing so hard that Mr. McDougall walked over to her and said she could stop.

"I must review your lines before you leave, however, Bonnie—and yours, too, Archie Johnson." Mr. McDougall examined the board with his grey-green eyes. "'I shall not play with...what? Play with *crows* in class?"

Bonnie looked. Yes, that's what she'd written—twice! Mr. McDougall would never believe that she was a good student who loved school. Sighing, she corrected her mistakes.

"That's better, Bonnie," Mr. McDougall said quietly. "You may both go now."

Bonnie and Archie were halfway down the aisle when their teacher added: "Pick up your sucker, Bonnie, and don't bring any more into the classroom. If you buy one at noon, leave it in your lunch pail in the cloakroom."

Bonnie could not believe her ears.

"Here, Archie," Bonnie mumbled, handing the green sucker to her friend. "I hope you like green."

"Oh, sure! I like any colour!"

Mr. McDougall smiled, but Bonnie was already halfway down the aisle, heading toward the girls' cloakroom.

Bonnie and Archie walked out onto the steps. "I'll have to take the shortcut, or I'll be late for chores," Archie said, his green candy bulging out his right cheek. "Sorry I can't walk the long way round with you. But you'll be okay." He clambered over the east rail fence and scampered off. Bonnie watched till he disappeared between the trees to the east of the school.

Bonnie drew her navy jacket close to her chest. The weather was turning colder every day. As she walked across the schoolyard to the front gate, she saw that Tom and Slinky were giving rides on the swing. Tom was making the children line up to take their turns. Betty and Tom's sister Ruth were up next, and two giggling girls from Grade Eight were standing behind them. Slinky was pulling on the dangling rope, not hard at the moment as little Freddie from Grade One was afraid to go too high

"Hello, Bonnie," Betty shouted. "C'mon and have a swing."

"No, thank you," said Bonnie. "I have to hurry home or I'll be late fetching the cows."

"Oh, c'mon, little milkmaid," Slinky said. "We won't make you wait your turn. You can go on the ride right away!"

"No, thank you…" Bonnie made a run for the gate but she wasn't fast enough. Tom ran and caught her in his iron grip. He dragged her over to the swing and made her throw her jacket on the ground.

Slinky had stopped the swing and was helping young Freddie get down. Then, with his big-mouthed grin, he held the seat down for Bonnie. "Crawl in, now!"

Bonnie stood firmly in front of the swing and did not move. She knew there was no escape, but she was not going to make it easy for them.

"Need some help, eh, milkmaid?" Tom sneered. The two bullies put an arm in each of hers and pushed her toward the seat.

"Sit!" Slinky snarled as he grabbed the dangling rope.

Bonnie decided she had no choice and so pushed her legs over the wooden seat and under the inverted V rope. She plopped down on the seat and grabbed the two sides of the rope triangle above her with shaking hands.

Then Slinky started to pull. At first, the swinging wasn't too bad. But soon she knew she was going far too high.

"Higher!" Tom shouted. "Take the high-and-mighty

higher!"

Bonnie took a fast look down at Slinky, who was now pulling the rope so hard that he was bent over toward the ground. "No!" she screamed. "No higher!"

"Higher!" came the shout from a few of the other boys.

"Higher! Higher!" A chorus rose up from the students standing around the swing.

Bonnie's whole body was shaking now, but she did not cry out again. She was using all her strength just to hang on. Her arms were being slashed by the leafless lower branches of the maple tree and some of the lighter branches were breaking off. Then larger branches started hitting her arms and legs. They stung like mad, and she was shaking so hard, she was afraid she was going to fall. She hung on with all the strength she could muster.

Then she heard a young girl's shrill voice screaming. "Stop! She's going to faint! Let her down!" It was Betty.

"Tom, you make Slinky stop or I'll tell Dad!" yelled Tom's sister, Pearl.

Slinky and Tom paid no attention. They were laughing too hard.

"Teacher's coming!" Pearl shouted.

Slinky suddenly let go of the rope, and the swing went diving down, twisting and turning in every direction.

Finally, the torture machine came to a stop. Bonnie sat there, dazed and dizzy. When she lifted her head, there was no one in sight. Bonnie's arms and legs were stinging. Deep lashes criss-crossed them even under the woollen stockings.

Bonnie stood up carefully. Then she wobbled over to where her jacket was still lying on the ground. At least it wasn't ruined. If she'd ripped that jacket, Mum would be angry. And she couldn't stand that right now.

She stumbled out of the schoolyard and slunk along the street. She prayed that she would get through the village without seeing any children at all. "Thank you, God," she said as she crossed the bridge over the Indian River. It seemed no one, not even an adult, was outside this late in the afternoon.

It was nearly dusk by the time she got to the edge of her farm. She climbed over the rail fence and found the cows exactly where they should have been. Their low mooing sounds were comforting as they trudged to the top of the steep hill. Then, across the pasture below, a streak of gold and cream came out of nowhere.

"Boots! Boots!" Bonnie shouted. He must have been watching for her. Bonnie kneeled down in front of her dog and buried her bruised arms in his thick coat.

NINE: BULLIES BULLIED

"What kept you?" Dad growled, as Bonnie limped into the barnyard. The cows were mooing to be milked, but Dad did not seem to notice them. He was looking at Bonnie's left ankle. "What happened to your ankle?"

Bonnie looked down. Her left ankle was swollen up big. She remembered now the stinging pain when that ankle had hit the main branch of the maple tree. But all the way home, it had felt numb. Now the pain was coming back.

"I...I..." Bonnie slumped to the ground.

Dad reached out and grabbed her by the shoulders. Dad cupped his hand lightly on the right side of Bonnie's face where the long lash mark had swelled. It went from ear to chin.

"Who did this?" he said quietly. "Tell me, Bonnie. What happened? I want to hear every detail. Don't leave out anything."

Bonnie wiped the tears out of her eyes with the back of her hand. "The...the swing..."

"What swing? Where?"

"In the schoolyard."

"How ever did you get all this on a swing?"

"They pushed me so high I hit all the branches on the maple tree!"

"Who pushed you?"

"Slinky. Tom and Slinky."

"And that's the whole story?"

"Yes."

"Well, I'm going to do something about this, Bonnie. No one is going to treat my daughter that way." Dad picked her up. "C'mon, now, let's get in the house. And I'll bring some cream for you to drink after I finish the chores. Eh? Would you like that? But maybe we won't tell your mother about the cream."

Dad carried Bonnie all the way to the house, with Boots running ahead and behind them like a bodyguard.

In the quiet kitchen, Mum was at the sewing machine, humming to herself as she worked at her favourite job. Then she looked up at her husband and daughter.

"Bonnie! What's happened to you?"

"Some kids' pranks gone wrong, Amy." Dad carried Bonnie into the pantry and sat her on the countertop with her feet hanging over the side.

Mum took Bonnie's jacket, shoes and stockings off. Her parents stared at the long, dark gashes on their daughter's arms and the bruises beginning on her legs.

"Where was your teacher all this time?" Dad asked.

"Pearl said he was coming, but I guess she just said that to stop the boys. I never saw him. I guess he was still cleaning the schoolhouse."

"But where were Angela and Archie? Don't they always walk you partway home?"

"Well, they had to hurry home and I was...kept...in..."

"Kept in?" Mum asked, wrinkling her forehead. "For what?"

"I was kind of talking in class," Bonnie said. She wasn't going to tell Mum about the candy.

"Well, this should teach you. If you'd not been talking, you would have been with the Johnsons and this would not have happened." Mum grimaced as she picked up the stockings Bonnie had been wearing. The wool threads were cut right through. "They're ruined," she said with a sigh.

"That's not her fault, Amy," Dad said. "Those boys will answer for their behaviour!"

"No, Dad!" cried Bonnie. "It won't happen again. I won't talk in class. Don't say anything to Mr. McDougall. Those bullies will just get worse if we tell on them."

"Bonnie's right, Thomas," said Mum, to her daughter's amazement. "Now, don't you do anything foolish. We have enough trouble, and these scrapes are only skin deep. Nothing to worry about. Bonnie'll be just fine after a good night's sleep."

Her mother carefully bathed Bonnie's arms, legs, and one cheek, applying iodine to the deeper cuts to stop any infection. Then she rubbed Bonnie's ankle with Rawleigh's Medicated Ointment and wound strips of an old flannel sheet around her legs and arms. With Mum's support, Bonnie made it upstairs.

Bonnie crawled in under her sheets. She wished she had a book to read, *Anne of Green Gables* or *Heidi*, but since she didn't, she'd make up her own story. She'd call it *The Schoolyard Revenge* by Bonnie Brown. But she didn't get past the first sentence before she closed her eyes. An hour later, her mother came up with a steaming bowl of thick tomato soup made from one of the few precious sealers of tomatoes she'd preserved at their old home. Beside it were two pieces of Grandma O'Carr's fruitcake, stored up from before the big move. But by then, Bonnie was fast asleep.

* * * *

Bonnie was dreaming she was sitting in Grandma Brown's armchair, right in the middle of the Belleville Library.

"Bonnie! Bonnie!" That did not sound like the librarian. "Time to get up, Bonnie!" Mum shouted from the foot of the steep back stairs.

As Bonnie sat up, she started remembering the day before. Then she looked down at her arms and legs. They were still terribly sore and ugly. She was not going to go to school today!

Mum started coming up the stairs. "Bonnie, you'll be late for school," she said as she walked up to the foot of Bonnie's bed.

"But you said I could stay home!"

"I said 'maybe.' We've decided it would be best for you to go to school. Your dad will take you in the wagon so you can rest your ankle. Then I'll come and bring you home in the wagon."

"I can't go!" Bonnie sniffled. "I can't face all those horrible kids, I can't…"

"Oh, yes, you can, young lady. So just pull yourself together. You can't let those bullies get the best of you. The more you act afraid, the worse they'll be. Just show them you aren't paying any attention to them. I know it's hard for you, but think of it as a small victory in a great battle each time you ignore them and act brave. Soon they'll find something else to do."

There was no winning an argument with Mum. Before long, Bonnie was on her way to school, sitting high on the wagon seat beside her father.

"You don't have to worry about those boys," he said, flipping the reins lightly on the horses' backs. "They'll not bother you again."

"Are you sure?" Bonnie asked.

"I'm sure," Dad said, his blue eyes gazing over the greyish meadows.

Just over the bridge going into Lang, Bonnie spotted Archie and Angela. "Stop, Dad! I can walk the rest of the way!" she cried.

Dad stopped the horses and Bonnie got down, very slowly.

* * * *

Dad was right. Tom and Slinky did not even look at Bonnie when she walked into the schoolyard. And when Bonnie began talking about her ankle with Betty, Tom's sister Pearl started talking about something else. But she offered Bonnie a piece of her horehound candy.

After school, Bonnie looked out to see if her mother was waiting for her with the wagon. She was not there. Had she completely forgotten? Bonnie stood waiting on the stoop.

"Better come with us," said Angela, when she saw Bonnie.

"Sometimes it's better to stick with your friends," said Archie. Bonnie smiled at him. In spite of his snakes, Archie was a friend.

Archie and Bonnie set off along the road where Mum would be coming with the wagon. Angela and Marianne walked on ahead, bending their heads against the cold wind.

"Have you heard any talk about my swing ride?" Bonnie asked, looking sideways at Archie.

"Yes, but not till this afternoon. Tom and Slinky were talking out behind the woodshed. I was on the other side of the shed, so they couldn't see me."

"What did they say?"

"It seems they're plenty scared."

"They're scared! Of what?"

"Of your father. They said he came down to Lang after dark last night and caught them both together. He threatened them within an inch of their lives if they ever laid a hand on you again."

Bonnie couldn't believe it. No one was ever afraid of her dad. Archie saw her face.

"It's true! If you could have heard them, you'd know they won't bother you ever again."

When they came to the Hubbs' farm, Archie said, "Here, I'll cut you a cane from that poplar sapling over there. Go fast, and you won't be so scared."

He took a jackknife out of his pocket and cut off a sturdy branch. Then he trimmed the side branches off so it looked a bit like a real walking stick.

"It's perfect," Bonnie said uncertainly. It was a bit crooked, and it didn't look like much of a defence against bullies.

Archie sighed, "Well, I guess I can walk you to the edge of your fields."

"Don't be silly," said Bonnie, pretending to be brave. She didn't want Archie to think she was a complete coward. "I can walk by myself until Mum comes in the wagon."

So Archie jumped the Hubbs' rail fence and ran toward home. Bonnie thought she heard him shout back to her, but the wind carried his words away. It didn't matter. She wasn't going to be afraid of those bullies anymore.

Just then Bonnie saw a wagon coming around the corner ahead and start down the road toward her. Sure enough, it was Mum in a cloud of dust.

"Sorry, I'm late," she said. "I was out helping your Dad in the barn and could hardly believe the time when I came inside." Dad's watch had stopped recently and there was no money for repairs just now.

Bonnie climbed up on the seat beside Mum. "Any more trouble with those boys?" she asked.

"No," said Bonnie glumly. "I just ignored them."

"Good for you, Bonnie! Better to face everyone bravely. I'd call that a victory!"

Bonnie was pleased Mum thought she was brave, but Bonnie wasn't so sure. She was just glad the day was over.

TEN: BLOOD ON THE SNOW

Bonnie woke to the same sound of howling wind and snow pelting against the window pane in her little hallway bedroom. Snow had started falling in early November, and in December the storms had increased. Now, it was Friday—Christmas Day—and it had been snowing since Tuesday afternoon. Would this relentless snow ever stop? She had missed Wednesday, the last school day before the holidays, and the afternoon concert. Dad had tried but just couldn't get the team to wallow through the deep snowbanks. "If a horse goes down in this, I can't help him," he had said. "We have to turn back."

Bonnie had sighed because her chance to recite the poem she'd practised was gone forever. But she said, "Thanks, anyway, Dad. You tried your best."

Archie had phoned that evening to say that the Johnsons were snowbound, too, but that Marianne's father had managed to take her for the concert. That was Wednesday evening, but since then, there was no news. The phone was dead. "Probably a line or pole down somewhere, and repair men couldn't get through," Dad had said. "Anyway, they'll probably fix it after the holiday."

Still, Bonnie was in high spirits. Christmas had always been a wonderful, magical time with lots of presents and fun with the big family gathering at the Brown's and all the happy aunts and uncles and cousins. Sometimes, weather permitting, they had made it north to the farm near Stirling where the O'Carrs lived. She knew there would be no relatives this year, but there would be presents. Mum always managed to make sure of that.

So now, on that early Christmas morning, Bonnie stared only a few minutes more at the snow-covered windowpane and then turned toward her parents' bedroom. The little coal-oil bracket lamp high on the wall, turned low, lighted Bonnie's way as she crept cautiously along the upper hallway. One step at a time, she tiptoed over to her parents' bedroom door to see if they were awake. Everything was quiet; so the way was clear to head downstairs and check for presents under the tree.

As she stepped around the sharp turn near the foot of the stairs, one foot slipped. She went the rest of the way on her seat, hitting the last few steps with a *thud, thud* sound.

"Bonnie, are you all right?" Mum called from the bedroom.

"What is it? The alarm clock going off?" Dad mumbled.

"No, Thomas...It's only five o'clock."

Bonnie's legs were stinging and her bottom was bruised. She knew she'd be in for it because she woke up Dad so early, even if on Christmas Day.

"I just slipped," Bonnie began when her mother peered down at her from the head of the stairs.

"Yes, we could hear you," Mum said dryly. "So now that we're all awake, we might as well get up!"

Her bruises forgotten, Bonnie flung open the door into the dining room. There was the sleek pine tree in the dark corner of the room over beside the phone. She stood staring while her eyes adjusted to the darkness.

Then Mum and Dad walked into the room—Mum in her housecoat and Dad in his pyjamas still. Mum lit a match, tipped up the shade on the coal-oil lamp, and lighting the wick, turned it up. The tree was more visible now; the light cast a glow on the silver tinsel and red bows she and Mum had put all over it.

But were there no presents? They must be hidden underneath!

But the old brown stocking she'd draped on the couch last night had something in it! A great big McIntosh apple was plugging the top. She pulled it out and dumped the rest on the couch.

"Be careful!" said Dad. "You don't want to break anything."

Bonnie sorted through her stocking gifts quickly. Three apples—saved, no doubt, from their Massassaga crop—and a few hard horehound candies. Two of the apples were partly shrivelled. Next, Bonnie found two new pencils and a brand-new box of crayons. She opened the lid and sniffed in the fresh smell.

"Look!" said Dad. "There's a parcel sitting right between the branches!"

Bonnie grabbed the small parcel. It had her name on it, but it was too soft to be a book. She pulled off the paper. It was a new scarf and a pair of mitts in striped shades of yellow, blue, and green.

"I used up all my leftover pieces," said Mum proudly. "You won't get those mixed up with anyone else's at school."

"That's for sure," said Bonnie. She smiled bravely, trying

hard to look thrilled. No one would know that Mum hadn't worked all these colours into them on purpose. The mitts matched exactly. "Great colours, Mum. I wish I could knit like you."

"You'll learn—one of these days," said Mum with a grin.

Then Bonnie picked a weird looking package from between thick branches near the bottom of the tree. "*To Amy from Thomas*," Bonnie read, and she passed the gift to Mum.

"Thomas, you shouldn't have," Mum protested. "You know I have no money to buy you anything."

"I know," said Dad. "Don't worry about it. I don't need anything."

Mum laughed a little as she looked at Dad's wrapping paper. It was old, yellowed newspaper tied together with binder twine. But Bonnie could tell she was pleased. Finally, the store box appeared and Mum opened it and drew out a pair of shiny brown leather shoes. She pulled them out and put her hand down inside one of them.

Mum sighed. "They're beautiful, Thomas." Then she took off her knitted slippers and, sure enough, the shoes fit perfectly.

"You've needed those for a long time," said Dad. "You shouldn't have had to put up with those shoes with holes in them. I used a bit of the cream money to get them. I just wish I could have gotten you a pair of stockings to go with them—those sheer ones with the seams down the back."

Bonnie wished now that she'd kept back some of that quarter to buy Christmas presents, but she'd spent five cents on one more trip to the store at noon hour. The rest she'd spent on two four-cent stamps, as well as two scribblers and one new pencil. The idea of writing her own book had really taken hold of her imagination, and she'd needed the supplies to get started.

"Well, I do have one surprise for you," said Mum. "I've been saving sugar. I'm going to make some cocoa fudge!"

"Maybe I could learn how to make fudge," said Bonnie. "Do you have a recipe?"

"Somewhere. But mostly, I just make it by guess and by golly! No, I'll make it, Bonnie. We don't have any sugar to waste."

Well, that would sweeten up the day a little! Mum's fudge was the best.

It was rare to see both her parents look happy. Bonnie was determined not to spoil it by complaining because she hadn't received even one book. But the house was so quiet—compared to all the other Christmases at the Browns'. She knew they'd all be laughing and joking and waiting for the turkey that would be roasting in the big oven.

She could almost smell it.

* * * *

Late that afternoon, Bonnie said, "Guess I'll take Boots to play in the field."

"Keep near the barn buildings in the sheltered areas," said her mother. "That snow is not done blowing yet. You don't want to get lost."

"I can't get lost in sight of house," said Bonnie. "Just leave a light in the window."

"Don't be crazy, child. You aren't staying out till dark."

Bonnie laughed as she and Boots ploughed into the deep snow and tracked out tunnel-like pathways in the big field in front of their house. Then a gust of wind would come up and nearly close them in. Still it was fun.

Finally, though, she sat down in a sheltered tunnel and hugged Boots around his golden collar.

"You're a great friend, Boots," Bonnie said aloud, "but now we must go back before Mum gets worrying."

Bonnie led the way through the sheltered barnyard but Boots whimpered uneasily and ran ahead as they came near the white picket fence around the house. When Bonnie reached the gate, she stopped in her tracks.

There were drops of blood on the snow! She looked back and saw a whole trail of blood leading from the barn toward the house.

Then Bonnie looked ahead. The blood-spattered trail went along through the open gate. That was strange. No one ever left that gate open. Dad was very strict about that. He didn't want farm animals getting into the dooryard.

As she pulled the gate shut, she saw more blood spots, leading right up to the front door. Dad must have caught something at last! And he'd killed it for supper. Maybe it was a wild turkey! They'd have a turkey, after all, for Christmas. Wasn't Dad the smartest! And he'd kept it all a secret.

She ran to the house. Instead of going in through the back shed, she followed the trail of blood right to the front door. If the butchered hen or rabbit could go in this way, so would she. Now, what would she find cooking? What would the surprise supper be?

Smiling, she flung back the door and stepped into the dining room—then stopped and stared.

Her father was lying on the floor, groaning. Blood oozed out of his overalls near the top of his left leg. The horrible smell of barn manure and human blood filled the room.

Mum was in the corner, turning the bell ringer round and round in an effort to make the phone work.

But just yesterday the phone had been dead.

Her father moaned again and Bonnie stared down. Like her father, she could not stand the sight of blood. She drew in her breath and looked over at her mother.

At last, her mother said, "Operator, this is an emergency! Please connect me to Dr. Wright!"

Bonnie sighed with relief. Mum had gotten through to the operator, but would she get the doctor? And who would get through the snowbanks to help?

Finally, Mum said, "It's an emergency, Doctor. My husband's been bitten by a sow. I can't get the bleeding to stop." Then she paused. "No, it's not excessive, but it's still flowing."

Bonnie slipped off her boots and rushed to the couch. She grabbed a cushion and, holding up her father's head, slid it under. Mum was still talking but Bonnie wasn't listening. She could only hear her father's low moans.

"Thanks...," Dad mumbled. Bonnie knelt beside him now. She forced herself to look down at the towel under his leg. The red spot was spreading out. Bonnie shivered.

Then Mum knelt beside them. "Dr. Wright's on his way. A farmer's bringing him."

"I doubt...if a sleigh can..." said Dad.

"Yes, he will get through. We'll trust God to answer our prayers," said Mum.

Mum got another clean towel and held it tightly over the wound. "Bonnie! Fill the big pan with water. Put it on the front of the stove. And the teakettle, too."

Bonnie hurried to follow her mother's orders.

"Now, Bonnie, take the oilcloth off the table. Can you get the extra table leaves to make the table long?"

Bonnie had to struggle to pull the table apart in order to set the leaves in place. She tried to be quick, but the leaves were heavy and awkward. At last, she got the final leaf in place and pushed against one end of the table. "They're all together," she panted. "But I can't get them to fit tight."

"That's all right. Later, we'll push them fast together. Now, I want you to fill the sink with hot water from the reservoir and pour some Lysol into it. Then, wash down the table with the Lysol water. Make sure you cover every inch. And wash your hands."

"Uggghhh," Dad was groaning more now. "I'd like to lie on the couch."

"No," said Mum. "Dr. Wright said you are to stay where you

103

are. You must stay still. He told me to keep this cloth firmly on the wound to stop the bleeding."

"Is it working?" asked Bonnie as she pushed the Lysol-drenched cloth across the table.

"Look, it's easing up." But Bonnie couldn't stand to look at her father anymore.

When Bonnie had finished with the table, her mother said, "Take off your dad's boots, but do it gently—start with his good leg."

"Bonnie…be careful," Dad groaned.

"Oh, Dad, I will. I promise. I'll be so careful." Bonnie's heart was beating very fast. She could hardly stand the smell of the blood. Her father's face was very pale now, and he groaned when Bonnie pulled the boot and sock off his bad leg.

Now all they could do was wait.

Bonnie got up and went to the window. How much longer would it take before the doctor showed? It was taking forever. Even the clock was moving slowly.

It was now five o'clock—suppertime in the winter. It had grown almost dark. Only the fire from the kitchen stove illuminated the room faintly.

"We're going to need stronger light when the doctor comes," said her mother. "Light two of the coal-oil lamps. Make sure the glass shade is clean and the wick trimmed straight across so that it'll give a good light. Be careful and don't hurry. Put one on top of the buffet and one by the pantry window." Bonnie lit a candle first to light her way to the shelf of lamps.

She had just finished when Boots started to bark.

"Let them in," said Mum.

Bonnie hurried out onto the verandah, and there was Dr. Wright climbing off the sleigh with his black bag. A tall, thick-set man whom she'd not seen before was tying his horses to the gate post.

The doctor rushed past her and into the house. Bonnie waited for the driver and followed him inside.

Dr. Wright had knelt beside her father and was examining his leg. "Clancy," he said, "we'll have to put him on the table. Nasty cuts—all three of them. He needs quite a few stitches. You did well, Mrs. Brown. You stopped the bleeding and got the table ready. Lots of boiled water, too, I trust."

"Uhhh," said Dad, when the doctor and his friend lifted him up and onto the table. "UHHHHH! Hurtin' terrible, Doc."

The doctor took a pair of scissors from his bag and cut the pant leg back. "Might just as well cut the pant leg clean around," said Mum. "I can sew it back on again."

Dad was still moaning.

"I'll soon stop your pain," said the doctor. "I've brought a little anaesthesia. Here, Mrs. Brown, I'm going to let you help me. But first we must both wash our hands in this disinfectant. Bring me a pan of water." Mum hurried back with the water and the doctor poured a little liquid from another bottle from his bag. "A little carbolic acid does the trick."

"Do you need me, Doc?" asked the farmer. Bonnie stared at the big man and saw he was looking as sickly as she felt.

"Not till I'm ready to go home."

"I can look in on the cows," he said.

"The two...on the west end...aren't milked yet," said Dad.

"I'll see to it," said the man, and he was gone.

"Now, Thomas," said Dr. Wright, who pulled out another bottle and a piece of fresh cloth, "just a whiff of this will put you to sleep and you won't feel a thing till I've got you all sewed up. Then I'll leave some pills to take away the pain when you wake up."

Crouched on the bottom step of the back stairs, Bonnie stared in silence, as the doctor gave Mum a face mask and put on one himself. He tipped a few drops from the bottle onto the cloth, which he'd laid over Dad's nose.

"You may need to do this for me before I finish," he said. Mum nodded.

Then a sickening smell filled the room. Bonnie gagged and backed up the stairs. She had to get away, but she left the door open in case Mum called her.

Bonnie sat shivering on the stool by her bed. After what seemed like a very long time, she heard the farmer's voice downstairs.

Then she heard the doctor's voice at the bottom of the stairs. "His bed's the place for him for the next few days. Glad you're here to help me, Clancy."

Bonnie darted into Mum and Dad's room and pulled back the sheets so that they could lay Dad down. "Good girl," said Mum, looking at the ready bed before ushering the men in.

The men came out quickly and headed down the stairs again with Mum behind, saying, "I feel awful to have brought you out on Christmas Day. And will you please start an account for us? I'm so sorry, but we don't have the money right now to pay you."

"No hurry at all," said the doctor. "And you know, Mrs. Brown, you would have made a good nurse."

"I always wanted to be a nurse," said Mum, "but—"

The hall door closed and Bonnie could hear only a mumble from below. She tiptoed back to the bedroom and stared down at her father's stone-white face. She choked back a sob.

Then she heard Mum scampering up the stairs. "Is the woodbox full?" she asked. "We're going to need to keep that stovepipe hot all night." It was Bonnie's chore to carry in wood from the woodhouse to the box behind the stove. It was especially important for it to be full at night.

"I'll put out some extra, too, on the pantry floor," Bonnie said as she ran down the stairs.

When Bonnie finished, she came back up to her parents' room. Her father was covered high with quilts.

"Is he all right, Mum?" Bonnie asked. "He's still so pale."

"Oh, yes. He'll be fine. It's the anaesthesia. It makes folks look like that. But look, there's a little colour creeping back into his cheeks. Go warm up the turnips for supper. And make your dad a cup of coffee with lots of sugar in it. He might like a few sips when he wakes up."

When Bonnie came back later, Dad was awake.

"It's paining…bad."

"Those pills will work soon," Mum said. "Just lie still so that you keep them down. Now, I need to check out things in the barn."

"Let that sow alone for tonight," said Dad. "I always take my pitchfork when I feed her. But today, I was hurrying and forgot. But feed the horses. And the cows will need some hay thrown down."

"Oh, I'll stay clear of that sow—never fear that!" Mum said. "Now, Bonnie's going to sit right here beside you. She's got coffee for you. It's sweetened and will give you a little strength."

"I can't take a thing."

"Well, Bonnie's here if you need anything."

Mum hurried away and Bonnie sank down onto the bedside stool.

"Dad...I'm so glad you're all right. I only wish...I could have given you something for Christmas. I could make something. You didn't get any presents at all and then...this happens." Bonnie was starting to sniffle.

"Don't fret, Bonnie. You were a great help. Doing all those things for me...taking off my boots, getting the table ready."

"You were in so much pain. I didn't think you knew what was happening."

"Oh, yes. Now your mother is going to need you even more before I'm on my feet again."

"Yes, yes, Dad. I'll try my best."

"That's my girl," said Dad and reached out his hand to place on top of Bonnie's. Then he closed his eyes and was asleep. But he didn't look so pale anymore and Bonnie could see he was breathing gently.

Bonnie sat very still. She supposed this was their worst

Christmas day but it had ended all right. Dad was going to be fine. Mum had found Bonnie a help—for once! And Dad had called her "my girl" again like he used to when she was little. And the doctor had made it over those enormous snowbanks to help Dad.

Things could have been a whole lot worse.

* * * *

Bang! Bang! Bang!

"Whoever could that be?" said Mum as she stepped briskly to the front of the house and turned the handle on the door.

It was late Monday morning, three days after Christmas, and someone was knocking on the front door. When Mum opened it, Bonnie could hardly believe her eyes. It was Grandpa O'Carr—Mum's father. His brown eyes were beaming from under his thick, snow-covered eyebrows, and his raccoon cap and coat were covered with snow.

"Grandpa!" shouted Bonnie rushing over and putting her arms around her grandfather's coat. He was just like a big, round Santa Claus.

He smiled and patted Bonnie's head. "I've got something for you in my car, young lady!"

Bonnie beamed.

"Well, Dad O'Carr," said her father, limping over behind Mum. "What a wonderful surprise! But how did you manage to get through? Seems the countryside is snowbound from Belleville to the North Pole!" The snow had stopped coming down on Christmas Day, but all roads weren't ploughed out yet.

"Well, the main roads are fine now, but these side ones are treacherous. I had to be careful. Good thing this old farmer can still afford a dependable car. It's parked at the road. I opened your gate but didn't start across that unploughed field."

"Come closer to the fire, Dad, and I'll put on the kettle," Mum urged.

"In a minute. I've got the car to unload and no time to waste—I have to leave by mid-afternoon to get back before the next storm hits. This sure is the land of hills, trees, and snow!"

"Now, Dad. I told you we need nothing," Mum said. "We're doing just fine."

Grandpa O'Carr looked around at the cosy room. In spite of the cold outside, it was warm and cheerful. He nodded with satisfaction. "I can see that, but your mother cooked up a storm and you're entitled to your share. The main part of my load is that old chicken incubator we pulled out of the attic. I thought we'd never need it again, but you know your mother. She's the original pack rat. And this time, she was right to save the thing."

Mum's eyes brightened. "The chicken incubator? That's wonderful! I'll hatch eggs nearer to spring and then I'll have chickens next year and eggs to sell. It sure will be nice to have a few cents of my own to spend."

"And eggs for baking—don't forget that," Grandpa said.

"But now, come out and hitch up your horses to the sleigh, Thomas. We need to haul the incubator up to the house!"

"I'm afraid he can't, Dad. He was wounded by that sow of ours on Christmas Day. I've been doing the chores since. I started to phone you but decided we could manage."

"Say no more. I'll hook up the team and fetch the things in. My car will have to be all right out by the road."

"I'm going with you," said Mum. "I can't wait to ask about everyone."

Bonnie watched out the window as they disappeared between the five-foot banks of snow on their way to the barn.

Bonnie was peeling a big turnip when a great clattering broke out at the front door. She plunked her peeling knife on the counter and rushed across the dining room to the front hall. A big gust of snow blew in through the door, and with it came Grandpa, Mum, and a big wood-and-metal thing.

"Where do you want me to set up this contraption, Amy?" Grandpa asked.

"In the front room," said Mum, shivering.

"Right you are…. Good thing the incubator will make its own heat."

Standing on the parlour floor, the incubator was almost as tall as Mum. Dad then went back to the front verandah and carried in a couple of smaller cardboard boxes. He was getting around fine in the house now, and planned today to start helping with the chores.

Grandpa O'Carr quickly unpacked the packages.

"Good. None of them broke," he said as he set together a

couple of lamps and chimneys. "You'll need these for sure. This room is as cold as a block of ice!" He smiled at Bonnie, who was watching with fascination, and motioned her to come closer. "Look!" He pulled out two trays just above the lamps. "We put the eggs in here. The lamps keep them warm and after a while, they hatch into fluffy little chicks."

Dad limped in with another armload of parcels. Bonnie took a basket from him and set it down on the hall table. She peeked under the fresh white cloth on top and nearly fell over with glee. The basket was filled to the brim with Grandma O'Carr's baking—cake, cookies, candy! What a feast! She scurried back to the kitchen so that no one would know she had been peeking.

Bonnie had just finished chopping up turnips when Grandpa O'Carr brought in another armload, which he set on the dining room table. Dad was still outside, bringing in the last of the gifts, and Mum was in the pantry with her back to the dining room. So Bonnie was the only one looking when Grandpa unwrapped the biggest parcel. Bonnie gasped with delight. It was one of Grandma's big red hams!

"Wow!" she said. "We haven't had—" She stopped and looked at Mum's back bent over the bread she was slicing.

"Don't you worry," Grandpa O'Carr said in a low voice. "I know you haven't had ham for a long time. That's why Grandma sent a big one! And look...there are some old bones in this bag for your new dog."

"Thank you, Grandpa! Boots will be so happy—all he gets is mash, usually. Thank you, thank you, thank you!"

Bonnie wished she could open the other parcels right away. But she knew she would just have to wait till Mum said it was the right time.

"These eggs aren't good for frying or boiling anymore," Grandpa told Mum, "but stored in a box full of sand in the cellar, they would keep well enough for baking for quite a while."

So Bonnie and Mum went down to the cellar to bury the eggs in the sand. Just as Bonnie was heading back to the cellar steps, she looked up at the beams holding up the floor above. There she saw one of those snakes. This one even flicked its tongue at her. Disgusted, Bonnie ran up the stairs. She hoped Mum would do the fetching after this.

Grandpa said, "Oh, yes. I've something else for you, Bonnie. Your Grandma Brown sent it to us in the mail. She was afraid the mail would not reach you in all this snow."

"She's right," said Mum. "No mail since last Monday, but thank goodness the phone's been working. What with the snow and holiday and all…"

Bonnie tore open the red wrapping paper. "*Anne of Green Gables!*" she exclaimed. "Oh! Thank you, Grandpa!" She barely noticed the new pair of socks dropping to the floor.

"That's not from us," Grandpa reminded Bonnie. "Look for a note inside."

"Well, thanks, for bringing it! I've wanted this book for soooo long."

Bonnie soon found the note.

Dearest Bonnie,

I was fortunate enough to meet Mrs. McDonald, alias L.M. Montgomery, when I was invited to tea with a group of authors in Belleville. After her talk, I went right up and asked her to autograph this book for you. She is a very gracious lady.

Love you as always, my dear one,

Grandma Brown

xxxxxxxoooooooo

P.S. As you can see, these socks are for your dad!

"Ohhhhh!" said Bonnie in awe as she flipped a page to find the signature. She hugged the book closely.

And poor Dad had a gift, too.

ELEVEN: AN ICY ADVENTURE

One early February morning, school was dismissed for first recess a little before the usual 10:30, and Bonnie rushed to get her brown woollen coat. In the cloakroom, she bumped right into Marianne and Angela.

"Let's go sliding on the pond across the road," said Marianne, pushing a wisp of her fair hair under her red wool cap. "There'll be lots of time."

Recess was supposed to be only fifteen minutes long, but Mr. McDougall had started giving them extra time. He said it was because it was too stuffy in the schoolhouse and the pupils needed lots of fresh air. Today, he was busy putting history notes on the blackboard; everyone hoped recess would be really long.

Marianne grabbed Angela's arm. "C'mon, Angela!" Then Marianne turned to Bonnie. "Let's go slide on the pond in front of the town hall."

Snowstorms had come so steadily that winter that there hadn't been too many times the ice pond was clear enough for a slide, but there was a breeze today. Perhaps, it would be clear. If not, maybe they could push the snow away.

The girls stepped outside into the bright sunshine. Archie was waiting on the bottom step of the stoop.

"Comin' to slide?" he asked. His eager, wind-burned face seemed even more freckled than usual.

Angela looked doubtful. "Mr. McDougall told us to stay

away from the river and *any* frozen water—even marshlands."

"Don't be cowards! If you were all boys, you wouldn't be afraid of sliding on a silly old pond. I always get stuck doing things with girls. One of these days, I'm really going to join the army, and then I'll be surrounded by brave men—like Dad was in the War—who aren't scared of ponds."

"Bonnie, won't you come?" said Marianne. "After all, it's only that little pond in the field across the road. No one can drown—even if they do fall in. Mr. McDougall really just wants us to stay away from the river."

Bonnie hesitated, "Well, I…" She didn't want to be the first to refuse. And anyway, a slide would be fun—just like Archie said.

"Oh, all right," Angela agreed with a cold stare at her brother. "If you have to slide, I guess the pond is safe enough."

Bonnie was not far behind Archie when she clambered up on the rail fence across the road, then jumped down onto the field in front of the town hall.

By the time they reached the pond, half of the school kids were there already, but they were not sliding—just looking everything over. There were a few snow-laden spruce branches from two nearby trees hanging over the ice. From these, the glistening snow was slowly melting and dripping onto the edge of the little pond. The wind had swept the pond clear of snow. It was a great place to slide.

Even Tom and Slinky were just staring—dazed by the bright sun. Bonnie was puzzled. They were generally the daredevils. So she hesitated. If they didn't slide, maybe…

116

But Archie was already onto the ice and skidding straight across to the other side. Turning around, he shouted, "Jeepers! It's swell! C'mon, Bonnie."

It did look like fun. There was Archie sliding back again. His cheeks were red now and his blond hair was blowing wildly around his face.

Bonnie stepped onto the pond very carefully, but Archie gave her a big grin as he reached her. So Bonnie did a fast twirl on the ice, and as Archie started across the ice again, Bonnie slid just behind him, her long blue scarf trailing behind her.

Bonnie and Archie slid smoothly but slowly across to the other side of the pond. Turning to face her, Archie said, "Let's go again. If we take a run at it, we'll go faster."

So together, they clambered up the bank on the far side and began the fast run.

On the opposite side, Marianne and Angela were also running toward the pond. "Golly! You can't have all the fun!" Marianne shouted. She hit the ice and slid, arms wide. Angela was right beside her.

Archie and Bonnie put on a burst of speed, hoping to whiz past the other two sliders coming in the other direction. Bonnie laughed aloud in anticipation. The ice was smoother and more slippery on this far side of the pond, and she was going like the wind when suddenly, just in front of Archie, it happened.

Marianne and Angela broke though the ice. They were sinking into the water with chunks of ice floating around them.

Bonnie and Archie flailed their arms in vain. But they could not stop. They slid over the floating, rubbery ice and splashed down into the big water hole—Archie first and Bonnie, grabbing his shoulders, following after.

Bonnie gasped as the shock of ice water hit her. Then she was standing in chest-high freezing water!

"Join...hands!" Angela croaked out between chattering teeth.

Together, the four victims waded through more breaking ice to the edge of the pond. Above them, on the fence, sat Slinky with a big smile on his face as a small crowd of kids gathered behind him.

"Looky here, guys—all the teacher's favourites!" Slinky, uncoiling his tall, lanky body, jumped off the fence and hurried toward the splashing group. "Now you're in for it!"

Yet he was looking at them with new respect in his green eyes. From the snow-covered ground, Slinky held out his hand and Angela took it. Then he fished Bonnie, still gasping, out of the water. Marianne and Archie managed to crawl out by themselves.

"We have to get home before we catch our death of pneumonia. C'mon!" Angela grabbed her brother by the arm. "We'll take the shortcut over the hill and through the woods. It'll be faster. The deep snow can't hurt our clothes, now. We're a mess already." Everyone knew they didn't usually take the shortcut over the winter months. It was a faster but harder trail and it didn't even pass by Marianne's house.

"It's too far to walk home in this cold!" said one of the kids in the crowd. "C'mon back to school and dry off by the stove."

Angela hesitated.

"Yeah," another voice piped up. "We want to hear what you'll say to the teacher!"

That settled it. They'd been playing on forbidden ground. Angela and Archie ran to the fence and headed down the main road.

Marianne didn't wait any longer. "I'm going home," she said. She ran ahead down the main street.

Bonnie hesitated a moment. At the other end of town, Marianne would be going by the road that curved to the right while Angela and Archie would go off the main road and take to the hilly path up through their own woods.

It didn't take Bonnie long to decide. She couldn't face going back to school alone and so she headed for home. Anyway, she'd have Marianne with her half the way if she could just catch up. She pelted down the main street of Lang after her friend.

The ice and water in Bonnie's boots sloshed and crunched and slowed her down. But she ran without stopping all the way through the village—past the stores, over the bridge, and along the Indian River road.

She still couldn't see Marianne. Where had she gone? Maybe she had stopped in at a house along the way. But none of them knew anyone well enough for that. Bonnie tried to run even faster.

Bonnie raced past the last village house and then rounded the turn in the road where the trees closed in around her. Her feet were heavy but she kept going.

The snowbanks on either side were deep, but the road itself was clear. She wished she had a shortcut through the woods, like Archie and Angela. But it was all she could do to keep going on the road. She hoped Angela and Archie were all right. Their route up the hill and through the woods was not an easy one.

Up—down—up—down. Her feet were growing heavier. She'd never go through heavy snowbanks. This was the only route for her.

Then Bonnie turned another corner in the road and stared in dismay.

Marianne lay in a crumpled heap in a deep snowbank by the side of the road.

Bonnie hurried over and grabbed her friend by the arm. "Marianne, what are you doing here?"

Marianne's eyes blinked open. "Rest—ing," she said and laid back in the snow and closed her eyes.

Bonnie knew she had to act quickly. "No, Marianne! You can't stop or you'll freeze." Her dad had told her about hypothermia when she was reading *Heidi*—a lot of the story took place in the snowy Alps of Switzerland.

Marianne started up but sank back again and snuggled deeper into the snowbank. "But...it's warmer..." She closed her eyes and sprawled out flat on her back—half covered with snow.

"Get up!" shouted Bonnie. She tugged Marianne by the arm till her eyes flickered open.

"Ouch! Are you trying to tear my arm off?"

"No," said Bonnie. "But you can't lie there, Marianne. You can't!"

But Marianne did not answer. Her eyes were closed again.

"Marianne, get up! Your body's tricking you. You just *feel* warm but you're actually freezing! Get up!"

What should she do? Bonnie's own feet felt frozen to the spot. Could she run ahead to the Hubbs' house just around another corner, or should she pull Marianne behind her? Would she even be able to do that? Possibly—for though Marianne was a fighter, she was skinny.

Bonnie tugged at both of Marianne's hands and at last pulled her friend to her feet.

"C'mon!" Bonnie commanded.

Bonnie pushed Marianne ahead of her and then grabbed the collar of her snowsuit—just in time—before Marianne took a nose dive forward. Bonnie clung to that collar and Marianne's right hand.

Finally, Marianne started to pick up one foot at a time. Bonnie held her hand tightly as they moved forward slowly.

Bonnie's teeth were chattering, but she kept talking to Marianne as they walked. "We have to get there…just around the corner…just around the corner…just…"

Step by step, they plodded on.

Finally, Marianne said, "Almost…almost…" Then the Hubbs' house came into sight. Turning into the Hubbs' lane, the girls staggered up to the house.

Marianne collapsed against the side door and slumped

down onto the doorstep.

Bonnie banged with her icy woollen mitts. Her fingers were too stiff to open the door. Just then, Rover the collie came bounding out of the shed. He whined and licked Marianne's face.

At last the door opened. The shocked face of Mrs. Hubbs stared down at them. "Maribelle," she screamed. "Come! Help!"

Bonnie stumbled inside onto the polished floor, her boots still on. Mrs. Hubbs and Maribelle dragged Marianne over the doorstep and started pulling off the lifeless girl's clothes.

Sitting on the mat struggling to take off her boots, Bonnie heard Marianne's weak voice. "Mama…I'm home."

"Yes, dear, and you're both going to be just fine. Maribelle, bring blankets."

Bonnie sighed with relief.

Out of her wet clothing and wrapped in a warm blanket, Bonnie was shivering less now, but soon felt pain in her hands and cheeks.

Maribelle and Marianne's mother carried the girls over to the couch a little closer to the wood stove but still a few feet away. Marianne was dazed for a while but soon recovered and sat up. Then Maribelle brought in lukewarm washcloths from the kitchen and laid them on the girls' worst spots.

"It's best not to get too close to the fire," explained Marianne's mother as she bent over, examining Bonnie's hands very carefully. "I think there are a few small spots that have been nipped by the frost. They'll heal. You'll see, dear."

Now, Marianne was groaning a little.

"My poor child, you were fortunate to have Bonnie drag you home. And how were you so clever, Bonnie, to know about such a thing as hypothermia?"

"Well, you see, I read this book about Heidi, who lived with her grandfather in the Alps of Switzerland. They had to be careful, too."

"Well, we're very grateful. You have saved Marianne's life."

"Oh, she would have gotten up anyway."

"Well, we'll never know."

"I feel fine now," said Bonnie, though she was still shivering a little. "I better start home. I don't want to be late."

"Nonsense, child. It's only noon now. If I can get through on our phone line, I'll ring your mother to tell her you're here and safe. Maybe the Johnsons phoned her. We wouldn't want her setting out for you when you're just fine."

Bonnie nodded gratefully.

"After I phone your mother, I'm going to make some warm soup for you girls. Goodness, child! I wouldn't dream of letting you walk home. My husband will harness the horse and take you in our best cutter." Then she turned to Maribelle. "Go find some of Marianne's dry clothes for Bonnie. She can't go home in a blanket."

Bonnie knew her clothes would be returned the next day in shipshape—all washed, starched, and ironed.

Two hours later, Mrs. Hubbs, Marianne, and Maribelle all were waving from the window as Mr. Hubbs tucked the buffalo robe around Bonnie on the cutter seat beside him

123

and set off. Bonnie waved back, and then as the cutter swept smoothly along, she kept wondering how she was going to explain all this to Mum. Mrs. Hubbs had not been able to get through to her, for the party line had been busy the whole time. Bonnie knew she'd have to confess every detail—even about their teacher telling them not to slide there.

Then Marianne's father cleared his throat and smiled down at the small form huddled in the big buffalo robe beside him. He was a small man but he looked big in his muskrat coat and hat. Bonnie looked up at him shyly.

"Don't worry, Bonnie," he said. "I'm going to explain to your parents how brave you've been this day and how you saved our Marianne."

Bonnie smiled. Now, she wasn't as worried. He'd called her brave. So maybe, Mum might think of this as another small victory. She sure hoped so. Nevertheless, she'd not be sliding on any ponds again soon!

TWELVE: BACK INTO THE COLD

After the warm, sunny day of the pond incident, a fierce wind began to blow, bringing more snow and constant cold for the next month. March had certainly come in like a lion, but would it go out like a lamb? Everyone quoted the rhyme, but as the snowfall continued, no one believed it.

Bonnie stared bleakly at the swirling whiteness outside the kitchen window. She could not believe how high the snow had grown in the field in front of the house. The zigzag pathway to the main road was like a snowploughed tunnel. As she turned away from the window, she heard her father stamping snow from his boots in the back shed.

Snow still clung to the bottom of Dad's heavy overalls and the cuffs of his red flannel shirt. His whole face was red with cold, and he even brushed snow from his eyebrows as he placed his knitted toque and mitts near the stove.

"You should have brought in your coat and boots," said Mum. "You don't want to take a chill, Thomas." She went into the back shed and brought his coat in, then pulled a chair over to the stove and flopped the big woolly coat over the back of the chair. Then she swung around and scooped a heaping bowl of hot oatmeal porridge from the stove. "Here you are. This'll warm your bones."

After Dad gave thanks to God for the food, he looked over at Bonnie. "I think you'd better stay home from school today. It's too blustery outside and it could get worse."

"Oh no!" Bonnie protested. "I can't miss school. I have a geography test today. I can't miss it. I can't. Please, Dad. Please, please, please take me to school."

Dad smiled over at Mum. "By George! Did you ever in your life see such a child? Most kids would want the occasional day off. But not this one! I can't understand it."

Mum smiled too. "Well, it's a good thing she does well in school, for I can't teach her a thing around the house. She takes no interest at all."

Bonnie sighed. Why did her mother have to bring this up now?

"I'm giving up teaching her to quilt," Mum went on. "She can't thread a needle, to start with. Then after I've threaded it for her, she pushes it up through the quilt—right into her finger. I can't understand how any child of mine can be so clumsy."

"But, Mum, I'm going to be a teacher when I grow up. I want to be a really, really good teacher. I'll help lots of pupils take two years in one! I don't want to be a house—"

Brrr-iiing! Brrr-brrr! A long and two shorts. Thank goodness—it was their ring. Mum flew over to the phone and took up the receiver. "Hello!" she said. "...Yes, Thomas is taking her to school.... Of course, he'll take them, too. Just a minute till I find out when he's leaving."

Mum turned to Dad. "The Danford children are wondering if they could have a ride with you if you're taking Bonnie to school. They say they have to go to Lang this afternoon and will bring Bonnie home with them."

126

"The Danfords? The new family that moved in next to the Stevenses'?"

"Yes, the ones with the little girl named Grace. They say they'll walk here."

"Tell them I have to go that way anyway, since the west lane is plugged solid. It'll take me about ten minutes to hitch the horses. So we can meet at the main road by our mailbox. If they start out in ten minutes, we'll meet there about the same time."

Mum repeated Dad's message as Dad hurried outside to get the horses. Then Mum started winding scarves around Bonnie's neck. There were only three scarves—a yellow one and a red one on top of Bonnie's usual blue one—but it felt like twenty. Hardly anything of Bonnie showed outside the snowsuit, toques, and scarves. Bound up in all those clothes, she waddled out the front door and struggled up into the sleigh beside Dad. Then she quickly got over onto the big sleigh box behind the front seat. Back there, she was protected from the wind.

As the sleigh headed straight across the field to the road, Bonnie nestled down into the straw Dad had piled there. Bonnie still felt cold but, just in time, Dad picked up a thick, old, black buffalo robe with a red lining from underneath his seat and, turning around, quickly flung it over Bonnie. Then off they went again with the horses' reins jingling.

Even across the field, the sleigh bounced up and down as they headed over the large, uneven snowbanks. Bonnie peeked out from underneath the buffalo robe. All she could see was the blistering white snow, so she ducked back under the robe, content to let her father steer the horses through the blizzard. It was warm down there; so she pulled the scarf off her mouth and nose. Breathing was easier.

In a short time, the horses came to a stop. The Danford children—two older boys and their young sister, Grace—hopped into the sleigh. Grace was only in Grade One but she looked even younger. She was shaking with the cold.

"C'mon under the robe with me," Bonnie called. The little girl crawled right in. Her cheeks were bright red with windburn and frozen tears. "You'll get nice and warm under here. You'll see," Bonnie said. They both lay on their stomachs in the straw. Their heads were raised slightly and their breath mingled and warmed the small air space under the buffalo robe.

"Gee, there!...Haw, I say, haw...You can make it.... Haw! Haw!" The girls caught only fragments of the commands as Dad directed the horses right and left. But they could feel every jerk, pitch, and sway of the sleigh.

"Are we...going...to...upset?" Grace gasped out.

Bonnie looked into the small girl's face. "Of course not." Then she put her arm around the little girl, who cuddled closer to her.

"It's more fun to ride in a sleigh than in a car because you get to go up and down. When you go for a sleigh ride down a hill, sometimes the bumps send you flying up in the air. Now you get all the fun of bumps but you don't have to worry about flying up in the air. Not with this heavy buffalo robe."

Grace sighed deeply and said no more. In fact, she was so quiet that Bonnie wondered if she had gone to sleep.

"Grace, are you awake?"

"Yes."

"Do you like school?"

"Most of the time. But it's a long way to walk. So cold."

Finally, the sleigh's motion smoothed out somewhat. Bonnie peeked out and sure enough, they were at the edge of Lang. Bonnie could hear many thumps, as more kids jumped onto the sleigh. Dad was laughing and saying, "Good job I brought a team instead of one horse and the cutter." Of course, Bonnie knew that the small sleigh could not have gotten through such high snowbanks without tipping over. It was not like Prince Edward County, where they used to live. The roads there were almost always cleared and even cars could get through the five miles to Belleville.

"The train stops here," shouted Dad. "All out!" He flung back the robe just in time for Bonnie to see Marianne and eight children from Lang jump off the back of the sleigh. Angela and Archie were nowhere in sight.

"Thank you for the ride, Mr. Brown," said Marianne.

Bonnie helped little Grace Danford jump down from the sleigh. The older brothers, who were supposed to take care of her, had run ahead. They were already halfway across the schoolyard. Bonnie couldn't help being annoyed with them, but she understood why they were impatient. Grace was slow and clumsy in her many layers of woollen clothes.

Slinky was sweeping off the pupils with a broom on the

front stoop. "Mr. McDougall's instructions," he said proudly as he whacked away.

"You don't need to knock my ear off," said Marianne, stepping back from the heavy-handed broom wielder. She gave him a poke with her fist and then ducked the broom as she swished inside. Grace got only one sweep and Bonnie was swept lightly as she pushed inside behind the others.

Archie and Angela were already inside, placing their mitts on the tin frame that ran all the way around the stove. Bonnie squeezed hers and Grace's mitts between Angela's and Archie's. Then Bonnie and her small charge hurried to their seats just in time for the opening exercises: the national anthem, "God Save the King," and "The Lord's Prayer."

As Bonnie looked around the room, she was surprised to see that a number of seats were empty. All the absentees were from Lang. Funny, she thought. They were so close to the school, they could have waded through the snowbanks if they'd really wanted to come. Bonnie shivered. The room was sheltered from the wind, but she could still hear it howling outside. The little box stove seemed to be struggling to keep the room warm.

"Archie, would you please put in some more kindling?" said Mr. McDougall. "I've left it there at the back of the room."

Archie looked sceptically up at the stovepipe as he opened the heavy front door of the little stove. It was red hot in two places. "Mr...." he said. "Mr. McDougall, I think..."

"Archie, just do as you're told. We need more heat. Classes, read your instructions on the blackboard. But Grade Ones, open your *Mary, John, and Peter* readers to page twenty. I will start with your reading lesson today." Mr. McDougall opened his own book and smiled as he watched the pupils in the front row open their books. Grace was the only one who couldn't find the spot. Her cold fingers were shaking and she was fumbling through the pages.

"There, Grace," said Mr. McDougall as he found the place for her. "Are your fingers so cold? You look warm enough."

"Mr. McDougall," Archie interrupted. "I don't think…"

"Archie!" the teacher shot back. "Do as you're told." Then he turned to Grace again.

"I have the place now. Thank you, Mr. McDougall," Grace mumbled in a tone not much louder than a whisper.

Archie grimaced as he threw in the rest of the kindling. Then he shut the damper on the stovepipe before walking to his seat.

"Archie, did you shut that damper?"

"Yes, sir."

"Open it up. There are cold children in here."

"But, Mr. McDougall, I don't think—"

"Archie!"

Archie trudged silently back to the stove and opened the damper. He gave Angela a worried look on the way back to his seat, but only Bonnie saw it.

"Grace," said Mr. McDougall. "What is the matter?"

The child had laid her head down on her arms. She raised her head a little and peeked up over her arms at the teacher. "I'm so cold…. I feel awful."

131

"Rest a bit, then," said Mr. McDougall. "It must have been that cold ride to school. And when your mitts are dry, you may put them on…. Bonnie, bring Grace's coat out of the cloakroom and put it beside the stove. When it warms up a little, she can put it on, as well."

The wind was still howling outside, but the little room was growing warmer and warmer. The sizzling smell of drying wool mittens filled the air. The children didn't think anything about the smell. They were used to it.

But then a great roaring noise rose above the sounds of reading, coughing, and sniffling. Every eye looked up at the stovepipe. It had turned completely red.

"Chimney fire!" Archie shouted as loudly as he could.

A mad scramble followed. Most pupils rushed to the cloakroom for their coats while a few of the older girls and the little Grade Ones looked to the teacher.

"Wait," Mr. McDougall said, clearing his throat.

Everyone turned around and stared at the teacher.

"The Grade Eights must help the Grade Ones. And no pushing as the rest of you leave. Just wait out in the side shed. The pipes'll burn out in no time. But just in case they don't, Tom, you call the men from the village. They'll be at Billy Weir's. Hurry!" Everyone knew there were always village men gathered around the pot-bellied stove at the General Store to swap stories on cold winter days. A few farmers often joined them, waiting for their oats to be ground for chop while they picked up a few supplies.

Outside, sparks were flying up into the air and onto the

roof, where they hissed out onto the thick coating of snow. The children were clustered in the schoolyard, looking like ice statues as they gazed up at the chimney. Only a few were wearing their mitts. Most had been too afraid of the roaring stove to pick them up, so they were trying to keep warm by putting their hands deep in their pockets.

Bonnie thought about all the school work she was planning to show the teacher that morning, and the book that she'd borrowed from the church library and had tucked inside her desk. She couldn't let anything happen to that book. It wasn't even hers. She started up the steps, but before she reached the door, Archie ran up behind and grabbed her.

"Are you crazy?" he asked, holding her arm firmly. "You can't go back in there." His hair was blowing furiously around his hatless head. His face was red with the cold. "The schoolhouse could burst into flames at any minute!"

"But it's only a stovepipe fire. We've had them before. They burn out once all the soot is gone."

"You can't be sure. Some of the sparks could have gotten into the chimney wall, or those hot pipes could break. If they do, those sparks will get a fire going fast in that classroom. It's all full of dry wooden desks and papers."

"That's why I have to get my things!" Bonnie said fiercely.

"You're not going in there, Bonnie. Anyway, the men will be here soon. They'll put the fire out." Bonnie could see that Archie was serious. He was also holding her arm in a vice-like grip. So she turned around and went back down the steps with him. Her cheeks were flushed as they joined the group again.

133

Archie kept his hand on her arm as though he was protecting her.

The jingle of bells filled the air as a sleigh came tearing across the snow-filled yard and stopped abruptly right in front of the school. Two sturdy men jumped off before it had come to a complete stop. Eight more followed once the horses stood still.

Marianne flew over to speak to her father, who happened to be one of the men at Mr. Weir's store. "We think it's only a chimney fire but it's a bad one. The pipes were red-hot and roaring!"

Two men tore up the steps while three raced around to the side of the school with a ladder. One of the three clambered up to the roof. The children huddled together and watched as the wind whirled around them.

"Seems to be all right up here," said the man on the ladder. "I can see where a few sparks landed but the snow was so deep they went out before catching fire. And there are no more sparks flying out of the chimney."

"I'd guess the fire's burned itself out," said one of the men at the foot of the ladder. "Thank God for that. It would have been a wild day to have the whole school on fire."

Just then, the men came out from inside the schoolhouse. "Well, that there chimney is burnt out. She'll cause no more trouble today."

"But it might not be wise to start her up too soon," said the other firefighter as he stepped down the school steps.

"You're right there, but what do we do with the young 'uns?

Their parents won't be comin' for 'em till the end of the school day and if the storm is over, they might not come at all. But we can't send them walkin' home now—in this!"

"Best put 'em up in the town hall till four o'clock," said Mr. Hubbs. "The teacher can leave a sign on the school door." Everyone knew that Mr. Hubbs was chairman of the school board. So they'd be headed for the town hall for sure and Bonnie was already looking forward to it. Maybe they'd even plan another concert like the Christmas one she had missed.

With the excitement over, the teacher made an announcement. "You may go back inside for your boots and lunches, and any books that you can carry and take home today. We will not be moving back into the schoolhouse until tomorrow morning. Move quickly, everyone!"

Back inside the school, Bonnie shuffled everything out of her desk and into her burlap bookbag. Mum had made it a few weeks ago out of a grain bag. At first, Bonnie hadn't liked it, but she had to admit it was strong. It would carry all her books, as well as the borrowed ones. Mum had also embroidered a beautiful big red peony on the front, which made it the envy of all the other girls.

Bonnie stuffed the bag full of her books and scribblers. What if there were still a few sparks around, smouldering away, ready to set the schoolhouse ablaze in the night? She wasn't taking any chances. After all, she was getting a ride home tonight with the Danfords, so it didn't matter if her bag was heavy.

Archie came up beside her and offered to carry the bag.

"Oh, thank you," she said and quickly held it out. Archie grimaced at the unexpected weight, then slung the bag over his shoulder like a sack of grain.

The students laughed and joked as they lumbered along through the snow. The wind was not blowing so hard now and they were thrilled to have an unexpected day off.

"Maybe we'll have a spelling bee," said Mr. McDougall. He was walking at the back with the slower Grade Ones.

"That's a great idea," exclaimed Bonnie. She might be picked last for baseball, but not for spelling.

Then, as she turned to smile at the teacher, relishing the thought of another win, she noticed something out of the corner of her eye.

Someone had fallen into the snow. It was a child, lying face-down in the frozen whiteness.

Bonnie ran back but the teacher reached his pupil first and was turning the child over.

It was little Grace Danford.

Her body was limp and motionless as Mr. McDougall knelt down to pick her up. Her face was as white as the snow in which she lay.

THIRTEEN: FEVER

The children trailed along in silence beside and behind Mr. McDougall now as he carried Grace across the schoolyard. At the gate, he stopped and looking down at the child, whose eyelids flickered open, he smiled kindly at her. Then he turned to his pupils.

"Tom," he said, "you run to Billy Weir's store and ask him to phone the Danfords and Dr. Wright. Tell them we'll be in the town hall."

Tom darted on ahead through the gate and across the street toward the General Store. The forlorn pupils tramped slowly across the road and around to the big fence that Slinky opened wide. Bonnie glanced briefly in the direction of the ice pond that was now completely covered in snow. Then the children filed up the half dozen steps and into the upstairs hallway of the old town hall.

It was almost as cold and chilly inside the frame building as it had been outside. The wind and snow buffeted the north-west side, letting cold drafts blow in around the windows. Siftings of snow had settled there and also over most of the wooden chairs.

"Go to the basement," said Mr. McDougall. "It'll be warmer."

They found a roaring wood fire in the pot-bellied stove and beside it sat Mr. Hubbs. "Well, I've got her going good," he said. "What have we here?" he added, when he saw Grace.

"Grace Danford fainted but she's come 'round. I sent Tom

137

to phone for her parents and the doctor."

"I'll go upstairs and wave them in when I see them coming," said Mr. Hubbs. He hurried up the steep stairs.

"Now, children," said Mr. McDougall. "We need a bed for Grace."

Lizzie spoke up. "We'll put chairs together." She and Angela dragged two chairs off the stacked heap of them, and it made just room enough for Grace's bed.

"Wait!" said Archie. He pulled off his coat and laid it on the chair. Grace's brothers stood frowning and motionless—almost as if in a daze.

"Thank you, Archie," said the teacher. He laid Grace very carefully onto the makeshift bed—coat and all. Then he wrapped her snugly on all sides with Archie's coat.

The whole class crowded around Grace. Her colour had come back, and her cheeks were even a little flushed now. The younger Danford boy started to whimper. His older brother wrapped an arm loosely around his shoulder.

"Boys, please go upstairs and watch with Mr. Hubbs," said Mr. McDougall. "We'll take good care of your sister." The older boy nodded to Mr. McDougall and pulled his brother gently by the hand.

Then Mr. McDougall looked over the straggly bunch—some with books and some without—and said, "Now, everyone, grab a chair from that stack and make rows over here. It'll be a make-shift classroom. We'll—"

"You aren't going to make us do school work, are you?" said Slinky.

138

"That's exactly what we are going to do. We can go over some of your memory verses. This is just the time. But keep your coats on."

Archie sat shivering. His big sister Lizzie took her coat off and handed it to Archie. But he shook his head and clasped both arms around himself. His face was almost as pale as Grace's.

Mr. McDougall stared at the irregular rows of chairs. All the grades were mixed up.

He sighed. "I've decided to read instead—as long as it's very quiet so that everyone can hear clearly." There was a somewhat low mumble of approval and so the teacher shuffled through his bag of books.

Bonnie hoped they'd be quiet—not that anyone was making a great noise at all, but a couple of Grade Ones were sniffling and coughing. Some of the others, like Archie, were shivering out loud, their teeth chattering. Pearl was sniffling into her handkerchief.

"Ah, just the book. *The Adventures of Sammy Jay* by Thornton W. Burgess." He glimpsed down at Grace and then took a chair a little distance away.

"Sammy Jay doesn't mind the cold of winter..." Mr. McDougall began. Bonnie settled into her chair. Soon she was lost in the world of the Green Meadows and the Green Forest where Sammy Jay liked to play pranks on his friends. Mr. McDougall read surprisingly well—Bonnie could almost imagine Sammy strutting around in his "handsome coat of blue, trimmed with white."

"Sammy Jay never seems really happy unless he is stirring up trouble for someone else," the teacher's voice rang out clearly in the little room that was gradually growing warmer and warmer. "He just delights in—"

"No, no!…Stay away!" screamed little Grace. Mr. McDougall rushed over to her side.

Grace was now sitting up and staring straight ahead in fear. "There's no one there. You're just fine," said Mr. McDougall very kindly. "Now, please lie down." He put his arm gently around Grace's small shoulders and helped her lie back. She seemed calmer now.

Clomp, clomp, clomp!

Mr. Hubbs led Dr. Wright down the stairs. "Where's the child?" he asked, opening his black bag.

"Right here, Doctor," said Mr. McDougall.

Dr. Wright bent over Grace. Then he squatted beside her, listened to her heart, and took her temperature under her arm. He stood up and shook his head as he mumbled something to the adults.

Then more steps were heard from above. "She's down there, Dad. They're all down here."

Then Mr. Danford flew down the stairs and rushed to his daughter. He knelt beside Grace and felt her forehead. "She's burnin' up—my little Grace is burnin' up." He stared at the doctor.

"Just leave her here for the moment," said Dr. Wright. "Mr. Danford, come upstairs. I want to give you medicine and instructions for her care. Mr. Hubbs, will you come as well?"

Most of the class sat very still and waited.

But Bonnie wiggled on her seat. This day had turned out to be nothing like a holiday. Unexpectedly, it had become horrible.

Mr. Danford came back with two blankets. After warming them for a short time by the stove, he wrapped them snugly around Grace and carried her back up the stairs.

Then Mr. Hubbs joined them again. He mumbled something to Mr. McDougall, who turned to the pupils. "The storm is passed and the sun is shining," he said. "I'm dismissing school for the day. You may leave for home now. Don't dawdle. One doesn't know when another storm might hit."

All the pupils clambered up the stairs in a rush. Marianne poked Bonnie. "C'mon and have a ride with us. Dad won't mind. At our house, you're still a heroine for bringing me home in the snow."

"Right," said Mr. Hubbs. "We'd be honoured to give you a ride—all the way home."

Bonnie and Marianne crowded together on the floor of the one-seater cutter, for the empty space beside Mr. Hubbs would be filled by Mrs. Hubbs, who was waiting at the General Store.

Riding backward now, they waved at their friends, who were straggling along in no hurry to reach home. A bright sun was shining and they were enjoying the walk.

"Best thing for all of us to be out in this fresh air," said Mr. Hubbs.

"What's the matter with Grace?" asked Marianne. "Is she

141

going to be all right?"

Mr. Hubbs hesitated. "We certainly hope so. Dr. Wright thinks she may have scarlet fever. He says there are a few cases in Peterborough. And the Danfords visited cousins there a couple of weeks ago."

* * * *

"How kind of you to bring Bonnie home," said Mum. "Won't you folks come in?"

"We dropped off my better half on the way over. Marianne and I have to get back to the chores. Now, don't fret about me bringing Bonnie home. It's a small kindness compared to her brave act of dragging my daughter home. Half frozen to death, she was! And she might have been dead if Bonnie hadn't helped her."

"Well, I'm thankful you've brought Bonnie home again. But I'm surprised that the children are out of school so early today. Is anything wrong?"

"Bonnie'll tell you all about it. Marianne and I have to get back home."

"Bye, Marianne, bye, Mr. Hubbs. Thanks for the ride!"

As soon as the Hubbs were gone, Bonnie stepped inside the dining room and exclaimed, "Poor little Grace is awful sick. Dr. Wright thinks it might be scarlet fever!"

Bonnie flopped her bag full of books onto the kitchen floor with a gasp.

"Scarlet fever!" Mum looked worried. Everyone feared

scarlet fever. The dreaded disease lasted six weeks or more and was worse than red measles. If the victim's temperature went too high, the person might be left deaf, blind, or brain-damaged. Or worse. "Poor little Grace. She's such a delicate child. We must pray for her."

"I could be next," Bonnie said. "I was so close to Grace. We kept warm under the buffalo robe together on the way to school."

"You'll be fine, Bonnie," said Mum, assuredly. "You were inoculated at your old school."

Bonnie wasn't so sure. "I missed the last three of those five needles," she reminded her mother. The two inoculations she'd had back in Massassaga had made her very sick. The second one had made her feel as if she were floating around the ceiling of the principal's office. Her teacher had laid her on the couch there to wait for Dad to fetch her home. Bonnie shuddered at the memory. If she got scarlet fever, would she feel like that for six weeks?

"I don't want to be sick again—not now!" Bonnie almost wailed.

"No one wants to be sick, Bonnie. And you may not be. Anyway, we'll face that when we have to." She bent to pick up Bonnie's bookbag. "Why on earth did you bring so many books home?"

So Bonnie related to her mother all the events of the day. "Some of the others heard Dr. Wright say that anyone with a fever would be under quarantine, along with their whole family, too."

"Quarantine!" Now Mum was worried again. Everyone knew how awful that was. The Medical Officer of Health gave you a cardboard poster that had to be nailed onto the front door to warn people to stay away. Only the father of the family could leave the home for food and bare necessities. Farm families could go around their barns and property, of course. In some ways, it was really easier for them.

"I'm worried about Archie," Bonnie said. "Grace slept on his coat. And anyway, he didn't look well. He couldn't stop shivering—like Grace."

"Go change out of your school clothes," Mum told Bonnie. "I'm going to phone Dr. Wright."

After supper that evening, Mum shared with Dad what she had discussed with Dr. Wright. She was so anxious, she forgot to send Bonnie out of the room. Bonnie tried to wash the dishes quietly, so that she could hear what was being said.

"He can't say if Bonnie's immune or not. Some of these inoculations are so new that even the doctors don't know much about them. Back in Massassaga, it was said that that serum was just an experiment."

Bonnie started to feel weak and shaky. It had been a frightening day. This topped it all.

"The children around here have not been inoculated at all," Mum added. "And Dr. Wright does not have any serum. There wouldn't be time anyway to do anything if this becomes an epidemic."

The plate Bonnie was holding slipped out of her soapy hands and hit the edge of the dishpan with a loud clatter.

Luckily, it didn't break, but Mum got up from the table.

"For goodness' sake, let me finish those, Bonnie, or I'll have no dishes left. You run along to bed, now."

Her words were brisk but she smiled at Bonnie. "Take a lamp up with you if you like. That overloaded bag of yours must have a book in it that you're dying to read."

That scared Bonnie more than anything else she'd heard so far. Mum must really be worried if she was encouraging Bonnie to read in bed.

Still, she wasn't going to miss her chance. After she'd changed into her nightgown, Bonnie sat up on her bed with a blanket wrapped around her shoulders and opened the book she'd borrowed from the church library. It was called *Little Women*; she was sure it would take her mind off school fires and scarlet fever.

FOURTEEN: ARCHIE

"Teenie may have it," confided Angela. "She's running a temperature. Mum's calling Dr. Wright today."

"Is she as pale as Grace was?"

"I don't know. Lizzie and I have been at Grandma and Grandpa Chapman's since the weekend. Mum phoned for us to stay there—in case Teenie has the fever. It's a closer walk to school, anyway."

"Is Archie there, too?" Bonnie asked.

"Hey...who's calling my name?"

"Speak of the devil, he's sure to appear!" said Marianne, joining the group.

Archie was not smiling, though. "Teenie is awful sick," he mumbled. "Mum's worried something terrible. I hope Dr. Wright gets there soon."

"His patients do cover a sixty-mile radius," said Marianne. Then looking at Archie's puckered brow, she added, "but he'll make it today—even if it's late. He always does."

Archie sat down in a seat opposite the girls. His cheeks were flushed and his eyes were slightly red. "Golly, Archie, you don't look so great," said Marianne.

"I'm fine. Just tired. Poor Teenie cried a lot last night. I'm worried—not sick!"

Not convinced, Lizzie spoke out. "You'd best tell Mum if you don't feel well and stay home tomorrow." She put a hand lightly on his forehead. "You don't *seem* hot. But your hair is sure a mess. Now, comb your hair."

"I said I'm *fine*!" yelled Archie. "Sisters! Jeepers! What I have to put up with sometimes!" He clattered over to his own desk and clapped his books down hard.

"What's got into him?" asked Marianne. She gave her head a scratch and patted down her hair.

"He's just worried about Teenie," Bonnie said loyally. "That's why he isn't acting like himself. Once she's better, he'll go back to being his old, nice self again."

Angela gave Bonnie a surprised stare. Bonnie added quickly, "That is, nice for a *boy*."

"Well, we're worried about Teenie, too," said Angela, "and we aren't yelling at anyone."

"My father says if there are enough cases, they'll close the school down," Marianne said.

Slinky wandered over to the little group. "How many's enough?" he asked eagerly, holding his hand over his forehead, as if in pain.

"I don't know," said Marianne, "and even if I did, I wouldn't tell *you*."

"Well, now, isn't that right friendly of you!"

"Get lost, Slinky," said Angela.

"Some thanks for pulling you out of that ice-pond!" said Slinky. He glanced quickly over at Bonnie and strolled over to look out the window.

Just then Mr. McDougall stood up behind his desk, grabbed the bell, and took it down the aisle to the door. He stepped through the vestibule to the outside door and rang it loudly in

147

the fresh air.

A cold draft blew into the classroom as all the pupils hurried over to stand beside their desks for opening exercises. Mr. McDougall wasn't stoking up the fire too much these days.

The morning dragged on with the usual lessons, but noon finally came. The pupils were allowed to stay inside to eat their lunches because it was very cold and windy. But the boys decided to go outside anyway. Mr. McDougall, as usual, walked home to his boarding house.

"How's *Little Women* coming along?" Angela asked. She was going to borrow it as soon as Bonnie was done.

Bonnie gulped. She was finished reading it, but she wasn't sure Angela would want it if she knew what happened. "One of the characters dies," she blurted out, "after the scarlet fever epidemic."

"Oh," said Angela.

"But she wasn't the main character—and pretty sickly, anyway," Bonnie assured her friend. "The rest of the book was really good. It made me think I'd like to write a book sometime."

"Lots of kids say they'll write a book, but they don't do it. Hardly anyone grows up to do what they plan to."

"Oh, I am definitely going to write a book," said Bonnie. "But it may not be published. I'll just write it all out in my scribbler."

"One scribbler won't be enough for a whole book!"

"Of course not. It would take at least five." Bonnie smiled at the thought.

"But what would you write about?"

"I don't know. Maybe about Lang School."

"Will we all be in your story?" asked Marianne, who'd just come up from behind and plunked herself down on the desk behind Bonnie and Angela. "Will I be in the story?"

"Of course," said Bonnie. "But if someone dies, it won't be you or Angela, I promise." Just then Mr. McDougall opened the door and marched up to his desk, snatched his bell, and headed back to the door. He rang it out loudly for the few stragglers.

The first bell always meant that classes would begin in ten minutes. The girls rushed to the girls' cloakroom to leave their lunch pails and line up for the washroom before class.

As the pupils filed back to their seats, Bonnie noticed the classroom was strangely quiet. She looked up at Mr. McDougall. He was staring down at his feet. Then he took a big, white handkerchief out of his back pocket and blew his nose.

"Little Grace has passed away," he told the class. The children stared at each other in horror. Angela put her head on her desk.

"Do you mean she's dead?" Slinky blurted out.

The teacher did not answer but looked past the boy as if he was in a daze. But Marianne jumped right out of her seat and went to the back of the room where Slinky was sitting. To everyone's surprise, she started whacking him on the side of the head with her scribbler.

Mr. McDougall was still staring ahead and didn't seem to

notice what was going on. Poor Slinky was holding his arms over his head, trying to protect himself. "I'm sorry," he said. "I shouldn't have said that. I didn't even think...I..."

"Start thinking!" Marianne shouted.

Knock! Knock! Knock! Mr. McDougall came out of his daze and walked down the aisle to open the door.

Dr. Wright stepped into the room. "Due to the scarlet fever epidemic," he announced in his booming voice, "this school will be closed until further notice." He soberly viewed the pupils. Bonnie felt his eyes stop on her. Thanks to her mother's phone call, he knew she had been huddled with Grace the day the little girl had fallen ill. Suddenly, Bonnie's head started to itch and she scratched it furiously—even with the doctor staring at her.

After a pause, the doctor resumed. "It is a sunny day and you may send the children home now, Mr. McDougall."

Dr. Wright turned to leave. He had only taken one step over the threshold when a voice shouted, "Doctor, sir, have you been to see Teenie yet?" The doctor stared down at Archie, who stumbled down the narrow aisle. "My sister, Teenie, she's so sick and Mum—"

Archie fell against the back desk.

Slinky and the doctor caught him and he fell to the floor in slow motion with their hands hanging onto his small frame. The doctor knelt over Archie and snapped open his bag. Then he waved some smelling salts across Archie's nose. Angela and Lizzie rushed down the aisle and crouched down beside their brother.

"Stay back," growled the doctor. "He's coming round. No need to spread this epidemic."

"But he's our brother!" said Lizzie.

Dr. Wright looked up then and recognized the Johnson children. "I'm headed to your residence now. You may come with me."

"We aren't staying at home. We've been at our grand-parents," explained Lizzie.

"Then I'll take Archie. Just fetch his coat."

Lizzie hesitated. Girls weren't allowed to go into the boys' cloakroom.

"I'll get it," said Slinky immediately.

With a low whimper, Angela turned away. Lizzie put her arm around her sister and they sat down together, staring with wide eyes as Slinky and the doctor helped Archie stand up and walk outside.

When Dr. Wright had gone and Slinky was back inside, Mr. McDougall seemed to come out of his daze.

"A quarantine," he said briskly, "is not a holiday. Since you already need to share textbooks in class, there just aren't enough to let you take them out. So this will be your assignment. Write a story about your time spent at home under quarantine. I hope that you will be a great help to your parents. Dismissed!"

A deep silence fell over the classroom as the pupils put their few books together, quietly slid out of their seats, and made their way to the cloakrooms.

Bonnie quickly dumped most of her books out of her

desk and into her bulging bookbag. Then she slung it over her shoulder and hurried to the girls' cloakroom. Who else besides Grace would be missing when they came back to school? Would it be her friend Archie? Surely not!

A tear trickling down her cheek, Bonnie bumped into Marianne, who grabbed her hand. Together, they ran in silence from the school.

FIFTEEN: QUARANTINE

"School's closed," Bonnie said, throwing off her shoes and galoshes in the back shed and stomping into the dining room in her stocking feet. She tossed her brown woollen coat and heavy bookbag onto the chair just inside the door and headed for the stove. She wiggled her toes and spread her bare, red hands out above the hot stove lids. They'd soon get too warm, she knew. But for now, the heat felt good.

"Of course, it's the fever," Mum said. She didn't quite hide the worry in her voice.

"Yes. And Archie and Teenie are real sick." Bonnie sighed. "I'll be next."

"P'shaw. You'll do nothing of the kind. But watch out for chilblains. You're warming up your hands too fast."

Bonnie went back to the chair at the door, sat on her coat, pulled the wide elastic braces off her shoulders, and struggled to take off her big, bulky snow pants.

"Now, Bonnie, I have a surprise in here for you!" Mum smiled down at her daughter as she opened the door into the cold hallway that led to the other side of the house.

Bonnie pattered along behind. She could feel the cold floor right through her wool stockings.

Then Mum opened the door into the front room. Bonnie had gotten used to the sight of the incubator, sitting right in the middle of the room with its own two coal-oil heaters on its open bottom half. Now Mum pulled out a tray halfway down the contraption. Bonnie looked inside. The tray, lined with a woolly cloth, was filled with rows and rows of eggs, each nestled into its own soft spot.

"Wow! Where did you get all those fresh eggs?"

"From our fine neighbours!" Mum started turning over the eggs with her nimble fingers. No sooner had she pushed in that tray before she had another pulled out and was busy turning each egg again.

"There must be a hundred eggs here," said Bonnie in wonder. "Do we need that many? Maybe we can eat a few." She thought longingly of fried eggs, boiled eggs, scrambled eggs.

"They won't all hatch," said Mum as she started turning the eggs in the next row of the second tray. "But by then, they'll be too old to eat."

"Why are you turning them over like that?"

"It's what hens do. They keep the eggs warm all over instead of in one place. I might ask you to do the turning some day, so watch me now. You have to be very careful."

Bonnie hoped she would *never* have to turn the eggs herself. What if she fumbled an egg and broke it? Mum would never forgive her. It would be like wasting a chicken, whose eggs could be sold. And when the chickens grew into fluffy, fat hens, they might finally have something else to eat besides sucker patties and turnips.

The phone rang—two longs and two shorts. It was the Johnsons' number. Mum rushed over to the phone.

"That's not our ring, Mum," said Bonnie. Then she saw

her mother shake her head as she placed her hand over the mouthpiece. Mum never listened in on the party line. But Bonnie knew the reason for this exception. After a few minutes, Mum quietly hung up the earpiece.

"Who's sick now?" Bonnie asked.

"Teenie, and Archie too," said Mum. "But Dr. Wright has left medicine."

"Will that make the fever go down?" Bonnie asked.

"Yes, aspirin will. But it won't cure the fever. It has to run its course. Mrs. Johnson is giving the baby sponge baths in cool water—several during the night. That'll reduce the fever. Some folks are afraid of using aspirin for babies."

"How's Archie doing?"

"He's not as sick as Teenie. It must be hard for everyone there without the older girls to help. They hope Lizzie and Angela won't catch it. Lizzie might just get set back enough to miss the entrance exams. They don't want that to happen."

"Lizzie was near Archie today! She'll get it anyway!"

"Bonnie, stop this fretting. Grace was a very frail child. Those are the ones that go out in an epidemic. The Johnsons are all healthy children. Even the baby is robust. Archie is strong from helping his father outside all the time. They'll be just fine. Now, let's think about all the cute, little chicks that we'll have in our front room."

"What if Mrs. Elmhirst decides to visit right when they're hatching—in her parlour!" said Bonnie.

Mum grinned and then Bonnie giggled. *Yes, that would be funny!*

Then Mum looked sober as she said, "Not much chance—not in this weather—and in a scarlet fever epidemic. And we'll have the chicks outside come spring. Your dad's building a special house—just for them. We'll take good care of our wee chicks. Just you wait to see how cute they'll be."

* * * *

After Bonnie proudly finished washing and drying the supper dishes without cracking a single one, she went into the dining room and stood next to the new quilt that Mum was busy stitching. It now spread over half of the dining room—between four narrow boards fastened together strongly in the corners with clamps. The top layer was a very pretty patchwork of spare pieces left over from Mum's previous work for the Belleville Orphanage—all pieced together. The underside was made of sturdy, dyed flour bags. The middle was warm wool from Grandpa O'Carr's sheep. The raw wool had been washed, dried, and carded into layered flat pieces that gave the quilt its thickness and warmth. Mum was very accomplished at any needlework.

"Well, Bonnie, I'd really like to try again to teach you to quilt. But maybe tonight is not the time. Would you like to read aloud for us?"

"Your quilt's going to be very pretty, Mum," Bonnie sighed, "but I'm glad you asked me to read instead. What'll I read?"

"Anything will do."

"Mr. McDougall started to read us *The Adventures of Sammy*

Jay by Thornton Burgess. But I don't have that book."

"You know, I think I do. Aunt Inez—your great aunt—used to give me a book every Christmas when I was young. Mum used to say they were a waste of time when I should be learning how to do things around the house, and an apron would've been more to the point. But Aunt Inez was a teacher, you know. So she liked books."

"I don't remember her."

"No, you wouldn't, since you never met her. She married—finally—and moved way out west. She was too busy reading books to catch herself a solid man for a husband. There aren't many good ones left when one reaches thirty. Mother says Aunt Inez and her family are as poor as church mice, now."

"Aren't we poor, too?"

"Yes, but no one knows it. There are different kinds of poor. That's one reason I'm glad we live in the country. No one knows how poor we are and there's always something to eat. Now, let's go see if I can find one of those Thornton Burgess books."

Together, Bonnie and her mother searched through the boxes stored in the big, cold room beside the egg-nesting parlour.

Bonnie was excited. "Mum! I didn't know you had all these books!"

"Guess I forgot," Mum replied. "Here's one about Reddy Fox. Didn't like it as well. He was always a threat to the other animals."

"I've found it!" Bonnie exclaimed with delight. She drew

out the beige hard-cover book with the black print at the top and the red trim. *SAMMY JAY* stood out in capital letters. In the bottom right hand corner, blocked off with a black line, were the words: *THE BEDTIME STORYBOOKS*.

When Dad came in, Bonnie rushed over to take the small pail of milk he brought in from the night's milking. "You're eager, tonight, Bonnie," he said, smiling.

"Guess what? Mum says I should read aloud!" Dad looked over at his wife, bent over her quilt. The *click, click* of needle against thimble was steady and fast.

"By George, Bonnie," Dad said, "that's a grand idea. I'm all ears."

So Bonnie began at the beginning of the story, but she darted a glance at her mother from time to time. Bonnie read on without a break for almost an hour.

"You know, Bonnie," said Mum, interrupting her daughter just after Bonnie had hesitated at the end of Chapter Twelve. "You do need to learn how to quilt. Then we'd finish here much faster. I do declare—I just don't know how you'll ever manage some day as a housewife."

"Maybe I won't be one," said Bonnie, staring thoughtfully at her mother, as she kept her finger at the spot she'd left off reading.

"Nonsense, child. All girls marry unless they're really plain or ugly. And most of *them* do, too. Ever heard the song, 'Can She Bake a Cherry Pie, Billy Boy?'"

"You're a bonnie lass," said Dad. "You'll marry young. How will you keep up to everything if you can't sew and cook and clean?"

"Or bake a cherry pie?" said Bonnie dully.

"You won't want to live in a dirty house, surely," said Mum. "You know what the Good Book says: 'Cleanliness is next to Godliness'!"

Bonnie didn't like the way the conversation was going. "May I continue reading?" she asked quietly.

Mum sighed. Her needle went clacking up and down against her thimble.

Dad said, "Keep reading, Bonnie." So Bonnie read until Dad's snores were so loud, she was forced to stop.

Mum stood up then, took a deep breath, and straightened her back. "It's past your bedtime, Bonnie."

"I won't be going to school tomorrow. So—"

"You can read for a little while more in bed, but at nine o'clock, I blow out that light. You're not going to be idle during this time at home, you know. You'll still have your chores to do and maybe yet, I'll teach you how to sew. Where there's a will, there's a way, I always say. Tomorrow, you'll be reading my pattern books."

Bonnie sighed as she walked up the steep stairs behind her mother. Mum set the lamp on the little stand by her bed and hurried back down.

Bonnie got into her nightdress and knelt beside her bed.

"Now, I lay me down to sleep, I pray..." She said the prayer she had been taught since she could talk. Then at the end, she added, "P.S. Please take care of all the kids sick with scarlet fever, and please look out especially for Teenie and Archie!"

* * * *

"Yes, Bonnie. You may phone Angela at her grandparents'. Here, I'll ring for you."

Finally, Mum had agreed to this. For a while, the party line seemed to be busy with calls for Dr. Wright and Miss Reid, his nurse—for their advice in treating scarlet fever patients. Then there'd been short calls between young women phoning their mothers for help and comfort as they cared for their sick children. Mum listened occasionally but never let Bonnie near the phone. "It's for emergencies only at a time like this," she said. "Not for silly kids' chattering." Bonnie didn't think she was silly, and she only wanted to ask about Archie and Teenie. But they already knew how they were, for Mum often listened on the line when the Johnsons' phone number rang. Mum hadn't phoned the Johnsons herself for fear the ringing would wake the poor baby and Archie, just when they might be dropping off to sleep. But now, Bonnie and Mum knew that the children's fever had broken a few days before.

"Hello, Mrs. Chapman. This is Bonnie Brown's mother. How are you today?" Bonnie was reaching for the phone but Mum motioned her away.

"Yes, that's true. It must be a very difficult time for you. And how are Teenie and Archie?...Well, that's good news. My Bonnie's wanting to speak with Angela...if she's free just now?"

After another minute or two, Mum handed the receiver

160

to Bonnie, who had to stand up on a chair to reach the mouthpiece.

"Hi, Angela! How's Archie?"

"He's weak but fine. So is Teenie. In fact, Mum can hardly keep her from creeping all over. It seems that babies get better faster than older children."

"Well, I'm glad. Tell Archie I can hardly wait to get back to school."

"Marianne says that's going to be soon. But Archie's not so ready for school yet."

Mum spoke up. "Don't hold up that line, Bonnie. Other folks may need to use it."

"Well, I'm glad it'll be soon," Bonnie continued. "I've got to say goodbye, now. It's been great talking, but we've been keeping up with Archie's progress anyway. Mum listens in every time your phone rings. Goodbye."

After Angela said goodbye, Bonnie hung up the phone to see her mother staring at her, a bit red-faced with embarrassment. "Bonnie, why on earth did you tell her I listen in on the phone?"

"Angela says it's okay. Everyone does it just to find out about Teenie and Archie. Her mother doesn't mind."

"Well, it matters to me. In the future, don't carry tales about home to school friends!"

* * * *

The classroom chatter stopped suddenly as Mr. McDougall motioned the pupils to stand for the opening exercises.

Almost everyone was glad to be back at school. The few who were missing were still recovering. Bonnie smiled over at Archie, who was looking well now—just a little thin. And Teenie was coming along fine, too, she'd heard. No one else had died, although Tom's sister Pearl and one of the boys were reported to have some hearing loss. Dr. Wright said they still could recover completely.

"Welcome back," said Mr. McDougall. Bonnie was pleased to see that the teacher seemed to really mean it.

Four weeks of quarantine were finally over. After the first couple of weeks, Mum had been satisfied that Bonnie would not take sick. Bonnie had been allowed to go outside once a day, making the long trek across the field to fetch the mail. She had thought this boring time at home would never end. She hadn't learned to quilt well as yet, but she'd tried.

So Bonnie was even more pleased at the teacher's next remark. "Now, before you hand in your assignments, I would like to hear a few of your stories. Who wants to read first?"

A few girls' hands flew into the air. So Bonnie decided to wait and not volunteer—at least not too soon. She didn't want to appear too eager.

She soon changed her mind about reading her story. Pearl had taken care of her sick mother. Betty had prepared all the meals while her mother cared for her sick father. Angela and Lizzie had helped their grandparents and prayed a lot for Archie and their sick baby sister. A short silence followed the last story. No other hands waved.

"Now, if there are no more volunteers, I'll just call out a

few names," said Mr. McDougall. Bonnie stuffed her scribbler underneath her desk and stared all around the room. She hoped the teacher would not notice her.

"Lawrence," said the teacher. A low groan was heard from the back of the room. But it was not Slinky. It was one of the two boys who sat next to him.

Mr. McDougall smiled. "So you didn't do your assignment, Lawrence."

Slinky scratched his head vigorously but was not abashed. "No, Mr. McDougall," he said in a solemn voice. "I was too busy taking care of the sick. My ma and pa were both sick and I had to get meals for all of us." Slinky's sister grew red and almost choked. The class all knew who had prepared all the meals, and it wasn't Slinky!

The teacher only smiled and turned to the younger pupils. "Bonnie, I'm surprised you aren't waving your hand. You may read yours, now."

Bonnie slowly pulled out her scribbler from under her desk. "Shall I read the story or the poems?"

"The story will do just fine...only *one* story."

"There wasn't much to write about," said Bonnie. "So I have only one story."

"Well, let's have it!"

"The Surprise Supper," said Bonnie impressively. Angela and Lizzie both looked perplexed, but Marianne appeared eager to hear her friend's story.

Bonnie felt a slight twinge of guilt. Though the story was true, it hadn't happened during the quarantine. She'd already told Archie all about the Christmas day accident, but she was sure he wouldn't tell on her.

Bonnie leafed through her book to find the story and said, "This is a true story."

Mr. McDougall sighed and mumbled, "Aren't they all." His words only reached a few at the front of the classroom. Then he yawned and leaned back in his chair.

From the blood on the snow to the smell of the anaesthesia, Bonnie filled in every detail. Then she read the conclusion.

"Dr. Wright told Mum she would have made a good nurse. She said she'd always wanted to be a nurse, but her parents wouldn't let her. They had a horrible, old-fashioned idea that nurses were not respectable.

"I told Mum that was wrong. I told her that when we were studying British history, our teacher had taught us that ever since the days of Florence Nightingale, nursing has been a most respected career for women."

Mr. McDougall sat upright. A pleased look spread across his face.

Bonnie continued, "'Can I do something to help now?' I asked.

"'Yes, Bonnie,' said my mother. 'I need you to care for your dad while I feed the cows and horses. I know I can count on you. You are always such a *great* help.'"

Suddenly, Archie laughed right out loud. The other pupils looked shocked. Mr. McDougall gave Archie such a cold stare that it wiped the smile off his face.

"So that's how I took care of my dad after his horrendous

accident. And that night the surprise supper was no supper at all. *The End*."

Every eye was wide open when Bonnie finished her story. Mr. McDougall said, "Fine, Bonnie. You actually woke up that back row of boys. That is an accomplishment. Now everyone, pass your scribblers along the aisle, and the end person can bring them to the front. Your arithmetic assignments are on the board. Get busy. We've a lot of catching up to do."

SIXTEEN: BUG TOWN KIDS

Winter had finally broken the last week of March. The great drifts of snow had gone fast in April as blustering winds swept through, and streams of water had trickled across the knolls and hills. This was one of those warm spring days in early May when it seemed more like June.

Inside the front room of the Browns' brick house, the eggs and the incubator were gone. At first, they had been replaced with many light-yellow balls of fuzz, scurrying and peeping on sheets of old newspaper spread over the hardwood floor in the front room. A little coal-oil stove had kept them warm. But by May, they had grown real feathers, and Mum and Bonnie had moved them to the little outside coop. Bonnie had to admit the chicks were really very cute in the fuzz stage. And even afterward, it was interesting to watch their wings grow in.

Bonnie smiled as she walked along the path to school. Things were looking up. Most of the pupils at the Lang school had accepted her now. Even Tom and Slinky were being nice sometimes, though they couldn't resist teasing her for being so bookish. Bonnie swung her blue tin lunch pail back and forth at her side and hurried ahead. Inside the school, Bonnie hung her coat on its nail in the girls' cloakroom and rushed to her desk before Mr. McDougall handed back assignments.

Opening exercises over, the pupils were finding it hard to settle into the routine. Slinky had already made one unnecessary trip to the pencil sharpener to gaze out the window across the fields. Then Tom had gone up twice. Finally, Archie made his way over there. The maples along the far fence were fuzzy with blossoms. Tiny leaves on the lilacs between the fence and road were starting to make a green curtain all along the edge of the schoolyard.

Even Angela was restless. Marianne was absent but her friend was whispering behind her speller to the girl in front of her. Only Lizzie and the two other girls in Grade Eight were working diligently. In a couple of months, they would have to try the entrance examinations. If they failed those exams, they would not get into high school.

Unlike the others, Bonnie was not gazing out the window, but her mind was many miles away—on Prince Edward Island. She'd finished her work but it was still spread out on her desk, and her pencil was still in her hand. She was dreaming about another "Anne" book that she'd hidden in her desk. *Anne of Avonlea* was the second in the series, and in it, Anne Shirley had grown up and become a teacher. She'd be a teacher—like Anne, not Mr. McDougall. It was easy to borrow these books now, for Mrs. Elmhirst had donated them to the little library at Keene United Church.

Bang! Bang! Bang! Someone was pounding on the door. Bonnie was suddenly alert.

Bang! Bang! Bang!

Everyone sat up and stared at the teacher. Even Mr. McDougall looked startled, and he got to his feet swiftly. But the door opened before he was even halfway down the aisle.

167

In burst Mr. Hubbs, Marianne's father. Everyone knew that he was the chairman of the school board. Even the restless pupils sat up straight at their desks and faced the front. Mr. Hubbs was a small, bald-headed man with a wide friendly face, but he did not look happy now. His face was aflame.

"Mr. Hubbs," the teacher said, his grey-green eyes clouding over with worry, "perhaps we can talk in the vestibule." The teacher tried to steer Mr. Hubbs away from the classroom.

The chairman of the school board shook off his arm. "I'm here for one reason only, Mr. McDougall, and the class might just as well hear it."

Mr. McDougall stood perfectly still and waited for the bad news.

"My daughter," Mr. Hubbs announced, clearing his throat, "has caught…HEAD LICE!"

How could Marianne have got head lice? Mrs. Hubbs was a stickler for cleanliness; everyone knew that, too. Bonnie had been to visit Marianne and had thought Mrs. Hubbs even cleaner than her own mother.

"We know where she got the lice," Mr. Hubbs answered their unspoken question. "She got them from this bunch— and it's a disgrace!"

A deadly silence settled over the classroom as everyone stared at the red-faced Mr. Hubbs. No one even moved a pencil or a scrap of paper on the desks. Then, in unison, it seemed, the pupils started to scratch their heads. Bonnie suddenly realized that her head was furiously itchy. Even Mr. McDougall raised his hand to his red-brown hair, but he lowered it before he actually scratched.

"Look at them!" Mr. Hubbs exploded. "They're all scratching away!...And you never noticed it? Man, have you no eyes in your head? This problem could have been caught in the bud. But now we have an epidemic on our hands!"

"I...uhh..." For once, Mr. McDougall was speechless.

"I'll tell you what you're going to do about it. You're going to march this lot—every last one of them—down to Keene. Dr. Wright will be in the office this afternoon. He and his nurse will examine everyone. A note will be sent home to tell parents how to treat head lice."

Mr. McDougall's face had flushed completely red but his voice had finally returned. "Is there a means of transportation for the younger students?"

"It's only *three* miles to Keene. The bigger ones can help the little ones. There's Tom there—a sturdy lad—he could take a Grade One pupil on his shoulders. And the Grade Eight girls could join hands and make seats for other little ones. These ruffians will be just fine. If they can carry cooties without complaint, they can carry other pupils. Have them take their lunches, too, and they can eat there before they come back."

"Everyone, you heard Mr. Hubbs. Put away your books. Get your lunch pails," said Mr. McDougall. "Be outside in three minutes."

Bonnie and all the other girls headed for their cloakroom and washroom. Once she was outside, Bonnie's head did not itch so badly. Maybe it was just the thought of creatures running around in her hair that had made her want to scratch.

Many were still scratching.

At first, everyone enjoyed the walk along the road to Keene. They'd been dreaming of getting outside, and now Mr. Hubbs had given them a holiday! Then the little ones began to lag behind, and the older ones had to help them along. Soon everyone's feet were dragging.

Over an hour later, they stumbled up the steps to the verandah in front of Dr. Wright's office. The younger children flopped right down on the unraked grass. Dr. Wright wasn't in, but Miss Reid got started.

"You might as well eat while you're waiting," Mr. McDougall told them. "This is going to take a while."

Bonnie pushed back the handles of her tin lunch pail and pried open the lid. She wasn't surprised by what she saw inside: two sandwiches of buttered bread and one suckerball. Archie was eating the same thing, so there was no chance of a trade. But after a few minutes, he offered her a donut.

Bonnie could hardly believe her luck. Mum never made donuts—they required grease, and they wouldn't have any until they could afford to kill a pig. This year's pigs would be sold in the fall, and the money used to pay the rent and some of the debt. That horrible debt took every spare cent.

As Bonnie was taking the last bite of her donut, Dr. Wright came bustling up the steps, right through the line-up.

He squeezed his blocky frame through the open doorway, past the line of children. "Sorry I'm late, Harriet," he said to his nurse. His strong voice carried out to the waiting children. "I've had a long night...visited old Mrs. Jones...she's gone now…then was called to the Maples' farm. Liza's had twins. That was a surprise to them, though I'd expected something different."

He threw his coat over a chair and rubbed his hands together. "So, onto this lice epidemic….Most homes have this problem from time to time, to be sure. Doesn't mean they aren't clean, of course. The way these critters crawl so fast, they spread like lightning—but we'll get rid of them soon. The girls must be reminded not to use each other's combs. Not much chance of the boys doing that," he laughed, "but they must be told not to exchange caps. Are we all ready?"

"I've set things up out here on the verandah so we don't get any critters inside."

"Well, let's get these children out of here before the sick folk arrive," he said.

Bonnie's turn finally arrived. She'd hoped she'd get the nurse but instead, she had to step up in front of the doctor, whose patience had become rather thin.

The doctor put two fingers to Bonnie's curls, rummaged around for a while, peering, and said brusquely, "Well, you do have lice. Next!"

Bonnie's heart sank.

The nurse handed Bonnie a sheet of paper which Bonnie started to read at once. It was all about how parents could treat their children's lice. The nurse gave Bonnie a little push, and she started down the steps of the verandah with Archie behind her. He was holding a sheet of paper too.

Soon all the Lang schoolchildren were strolling back to the

main road that led through Keene toward home. Some were still eating their lunches while others had lost their appetites. Most of the Grade Ones were whimpering about their heads itching and their feet hurting.

The thought of the dreadful insects crawling all around her head made Bonnie shudder. That spring, Bonnie had been left to comb her own hair each morning. She had liked that because she didn't pull out the tangles as hard as her mother did. But now all that would change. Mum would be inspecting her head—and those instructions did not sound like fun.

Mr. McDougall and Mr. Hubbs were no longer in sight, so the Lang schoolchildren walked on slowly in a silent, solemn way. No one felt like talking. Everyone was glum—even Slinky and Tom.

The Keene pupils were outside playing and watching a baseball game when the bedraggled bunch from Lang School passed by them. They stopped playing to stare with curiosity.

"I'm thirsty!" a Grade One pupil grumbled. This set off a whole chorus of requests.

"Well, I do declare," said Slinky. "I think I spy a pump; don't you, Tom?"

"Yes, I do. C'mon, kids. There's water enough here for everyone."

Tom and Slinky led the way through the narrow gate and into the Keene schoolyard. Tom pumped water for everyone. Most of the pupils had empty cups in their lunch boxes and some shared their cups with the others who had none. The fresh well water tasted very good to the thirsty travellers.

"Come on, Bonnie," Tom said. "You can have a drink too."

Bonnie wasn't sure. She might be on better terms with these boys now, but she still remembered the day Tom and Slinky had showered her with pump water at school. She plucked up enough courage to look Tom in the eye. There was no smirk on his face. He looked at Bonnie and said quietly, so no one else would hear, "Here, give me your cup."

She fished in her lunch pail and handed it to him. He filled it with water and handed it back. Bonnie took long, deep gulps of the fresh, cold water.

"Next!" Tom said.

When Bonnie turned from the well, she gasped. Two rows of Keene pupils had circled around the children at the pump. The bigger boys began shouting, "Get out, you Lang kids! Get out! We don't want your cooties!"

Bonnie could hardly believe her ears. How fast the news had spread!

The jeers were getting louder. "Yeah, get out, cootie kids! Go home to your own town—*Bug town, bug town, bug town kids. Bug town, Lang town, on the skids!*"

Their loud jeering was suddenly overwhelmed by the heavy rattling of their teacher's bell. Instantly, the Keene pupils turned and ran toward the open door where their teacher stood scowling at them.

The Lang kids moved away from the pump and went back to the road. Some looked at their toes and some blushed with shame. Even Slinky and Tom had nothing to say. The journey back to the Lang school seemed twice as far as the walk from

Lang to Keene.

Finally, at three o'clock, the stragglers turned off the gravel road and onto the dust-packed route that led into the village of Lang.

When Tom opened the door to the school, there was Mr. McDougall, marking papers at his desk as if nothing had happened. Every eye looked at him resentfully. He had taken a ride back and left the pupils to fend for themselves. But he returned their looks with his own look of disgust on his face. Utterly demoralized, the children slunk to their seats in silence.

"It seems that there are only five pupils—two from Grade One and three girls from Grade Eight—who do not have head lice," Mr. McDougall said. "Each of you who has been diagnosed with lice must take home the sheet you received from Dr. Wright. I have extras here in case any of you lost your sheets on the way back. Your parents must follow the instructions on the sheet and start your treatment this evening."

He attempted a joke next—probably to lighten the atmosphere of doom and gloom that had settled over the classroom. "Tomorrow will be Lice Day," he said. And then he chuckled.

No one even smiled.

Mr. McDougall cleared his throat and went on, "After our National Anthem, you will walk to Keene for inspection by the medical officer of health. This is not my instruction. It is the law! So tell your parents. There can be no truants. Those

174

without lice may stay at home or remain here to work on their own while the rest are going to Keene."

Mr. McDougall sat down and several hands flew up in the air.

"Well, what is it?" Mr. McDougall sounded irritated.

"Will we go just the once or more often?" asked Angela.

"Each of you must be examined every day until you are free of lice. For now, follow the instructions on the sheet. Don't use each other's combs or wear anyone else's hat. And don't sit too near each other. Lice can jump from one head to another if they are not far apart."

"But we share desks and even books," said Tom, without even raising his hand.

Mr. McDougall just shrugged, unconcerned.

SEVENTEEN: SHORN

"Mum, where are you?" Bonnie called as she stepped through the back door and into the log shed—their summer kitchen. The dining room was used only for company, now, and since the chickens had been moved out of the parlour, Mum had unpacked her good furniture. So they finally had two nice rooms in the house.

"I'm up here, Bonnie!" Mum was upstairs, cleaning out the winter bedrooms. They would be sleeping in the cooler and the more spacious front bedrooms during the summer.

"I have something important to show you, Mum."

"Can't it keep? I'm awfully busy."

"I suppose." Bonnie plopped the sheet down on the kitchen table. She was not looking forward to telling her mother about the head lice. Well, she had to do her chores first, anyway. So she called Boots and headed out to bring in the cows.

When she got back, Mum was reading the sheet about the lice. "I can't believe my eyes," she said. "Do you have lice, Bonnie?"

"Most everybody does," Bonnie squeaked.

"You must have been using someone else's comb. How many times have I told you not to use anyone else's comb!"

"But I didn't. Honest. Our teacher says lice can jump from one head to another. So I guess one must have jumped onto me from someone else's head. Our desks are so close together."

"Nonsense! That's an old wives' tale. Lice don't jump or

fly—but they do scurry. You must have had your head right next to someone else's or shared a hat. Don't get too thick with those Lang kids. I'll bet the Hubbs and Johnsons don't have lice!"

"Yes, they do. That's how we found out. Mr. Hubbs came to the school because Marianne has lice. Then he sent us all down to Keene to be checked."

Mum shook her head. "Well, don't just stand there. Come over here and let me take a look."

Bonnie stood still as her mother parted her curls. "Here they are…" Mum said. "Little white clumps on each strand. And some of the wretched creatures are walking brazenly along your hair as if they own it. And—" Mum dropped the strands of hair she'd been holding as if she'd been burned. "More of them, actually laying eggs! What a mess! You're covered with lice and nits!"

Bonnie shuddered and nearly threw up. She no longer cared how unpleasant the treatment might be. She wanted those horrible things out!

"Go back into the outer shed and take off all your clothes," said Mum. "I'll bring you out an old housecoat to put on after you bathe. No point in bathing, though, till after we get you doused with coal oil. Some of it's bound to drip down."

Just beyond the summer kitchen was another roofed area, closed on three sides but open to the south. It was almost like being outside, and Bonnie felt strange, though she knew no one could possibly see into this sheltered area away from the front of the house.

177

Bonnie stripped, then stood, shaking and fearful. A fresh breeze was blowing in, and Bonnie started coughing. She hadn't had a coughing fit for a long, long time. She didn't even have a towel to cover herself up, since Mum didn't want her to touch anything for fear of spreading the lice. Mum yanked a big square tin tub off the wall.

"Won't the lice get on the tub?" asked Bonnie.

"They can't live on tin," said Mum. "And, anyway, don't worry. I'll clean it afterward. We'll also have to clean everything in this house. We'll use the copper boiler on the stove for all the bedding, towels, and all your clothes. It's the only way to kill the eggs. Now, walk out to the grass. I don't want this coal oil inside the shed. It could start a fire. Close your eyes and keep them closed."

Bonnie closed her eyes and squinted. She knew the coal oil would hurt when it reached her head. She waited and waited. Then she realized what was happening. Mum was *cutting* her hair!

"Mum!" Bonnie shrieked, stepping back and opening her eyes. "What are you doing?"

"I'm cutting your hair," Mum said calmly. "It's so matted that the coal oil won't get through properly. You'll thank me later. Your head will be sore enough from the coal oil and lye soap without my pulling on those tangles." She continued to snip away at Bonnie's hair.

"Don't take it all!" Bonnie begged.

"I won't. My goodness, I've got the scissors here—not your father's razor. Don't worry, the short ends will curl and you'll

178

look just fine. I hate to think what the kids with straight hair will look like."

Bonnie looked down at the ground as chunks of her dark golden curls fell on the floor. It seemed like a lot of hair. How could she possibly look good after this? But she would not be completely bald, like the boys.

"Now close your eyes," Mum said gruffly.

Bonnie gasped as the coal oil hit her head. She'd been scratching and the raw spots were sensitive. They started to sting terribly. Soon her whole head was aflame. But at least the itching had stopped.

Bonnie kept her eyes shut tightly as Mum led her back into the inner shed. "Stand here and keep your eyes shut. I'll fill the tub with nice, warm water from the reservoir."

After waiting in the chilly air for what seemed like months, Bonnie took Mum's hand and stepped up and over the side of the tub. She had to cross her ankles and bend her knees to fit, but once she got into the water, it was a nice feeling. Mum gave her a washcloth to put over her eyes.

"While you're soaking, I'll strip your bed and gather up all your clothes. With luck and this wind, your sheets should be dry by bedtime."

Half an hour later, Mum returned with hot water to warm up the tub. Then she applied strong lye soap to Bonnie's short hair and scrubbed hard—pushing Bonnie's head back and forth. When she thought she'd scrubbed enough, she poured fresh water from a nearby pan over Bonnie's head. Then she told her to step up and into another tub of fresh rinse water.

"Just like Monday wash day, Bonnie—wash water, then rinse water." Bonnie's face was stinging, and the clear water of the second tub didn't stop the pain. Little blisters were bursting out over her hairline and in patches on her face. The only thing worse, Bonnie thought, would be bluing. It's a wonder Mum didn't add some of that to make her cleaner and whiter! But maybe her mother could see that she was blue enough!

It was a long evening. All the sheets were plunged into the copper boiler on the stove, then rinsed in two tubs that had been disinfected first with coal oil and then with Lysol. Then the sheets were hung on the line outside.

When Mum tucked Bonnie in for the night, the sheets on her bed were crisp and white, and a thick towel lay on her pillow to protect it from the light coating of coal oil Mum had reapplied to Bonnie's hair. "Enough to kill any lice that hatch during the night," Mum said.

"How long is this going to go on?" Bonnie asked. The smell of coal oil was making her sick.

"Probably a week. That should finish them off. Your father and I will have to check each other for lice when he comes in from the barn. He's taking the time to clean out the horse stable. You know how fussy he is. He likes to keep the barns as clean as I keep the house." Mum said it with a laugh, but Bonnie knew she was bragging a little about Dad. She also knew how angry he'd be if he had lice. Would he blame her?

Bonnie sighed and closed her eyes. How could she ever sleep with the coal oil smell all around her? But soon she was thinking of something else. Those Keene kids and their rude taunts! Then she smiled.

Before she fell asleep, she had a plan.

EIGHTEEN: BONNIE'S PLAN

The Lang school kids were a sorry sight as they straggled toward the outskirts of Keene. Most of the boys were bald. All the girls had short-clipped hair.

Bonnie's hair looked all right, for the ends had curled and no thin spots were showing. But Bonnie's face was another matter. It was a mess of blisters around the hairline and across one cheek.

Of all the pupils, Archie looked the worst. He had no hair left and there were blisters all over his head and face. Angela didn't have any blisters, but her straight dark hair stuck out in all directions. Lizzie was one of the lucky ones. She didn't have lice, so she'd stayed at the schoolhouse with the two other Grade Eight girls and the two Grade One students. Mr. McDougall would be teaching them today while the others took the long walk to Keene.

Bonnie was wearing an old pair of navy blue slacks and a shirt that had been made over so often it was almost completely covered with patches. All her other clothes were still drying. Her head was sore, both outside and in, for she couldn't stop thinking about the horrible kids at the Keene school. What would they be yelling when they saw this sorry parade heading into the village today?

Archie seemed to be reading Bonnie's thoughts. "The Keene kids will be out in the schoolyard when we go by," he said. "It will be recess by the time we get there."

"Well," said Bonnie. "I've got a rhyme ready for them if they yell at us again."

"Poetry!" Slinky growled. "No poem is gonna help! Those guys need a punch in the nose!"

"We can't do that," said Archie, "or we'll be in more trouble. Let's see your rhyme, Bonnie."

Slinky snorted but made no trouble. He was feeling too miserable to do anything but put one foot ahead of the other.

"This is really good," said Archie. He waved the paper around. "Hey, everybody! Look at Bonnie's poem! It's perfect."

Slinky grabbed the poem from Archie's hand. "Let's see that thing!" As Slinky read, he seemed to come back to life again. He grabbed Bonnie's hand and raised it in the air. "This girl is a great poet!" he shouted.

Then Slinky passed the paper down the line. The children mumbled the words under their breath so they'd remember them.

"Bonnie will lead us," said Slinky, dropping her hand and standing beside her in the middle of the group. "Let's practise."

Bonnie shouted out the words and the children repeated them after her. Then she and Slinky led the troops the rest of the way to Keene. Everyone was in much better spirits. And now they were actually hoping the Keene school kids would say nasty things to them.

When they reached the edge of the village, they heard a tiny voice screaming from behind a bush, "Here come the Cootie Kids from Bug Town!"

"Not yet!" said Slinky, putting up his hand like a police

183

officer. "He's only a little kid."

Grim-faced, they plodded on. In a few minutes, the school appeared before them. The yard was filled with kids. "Be ready," Slinky said quietly, "but let them go first." This was a new Slinky.

Bonnie was still at the head of the line, now flanked by Archie and Slinky. The Lang kids looked straight ahead. Even the Grade Ones resisted looking over at the schoolyard.

Then it started. The Keene kids stopped their baseball game and started climbing up the fence that lined the street. Two boys hung down from a maple tree at the edge of the schoolyard. "Here come the Cootie Kids from Bug Town!" they yelled. "Cootie Kids from Bug Town!" the shouters kept repeating.

Bonnie looked straight at them. A mighty roar swelled above the name calling. The Lang school kids were shouting her poem at the top of their voices.

"Beware of our Cooties,
Fear our disease,
We'll sting you like hornets,
We'll bite you like fleas,
And if you don't want to die,
Then you'd better just freeze!
Freeze! Freeze! Freeze!"

They marched on, holding their heads high and shouting her poem over and over again. They were so loud that they drowned out the sound of the Keene school bell ringing the pupils back into class. When they finally turned left into Dr.

Wright's street, they stopped shouting.

They were a more confident group now as they stepped briskly down the street and then onto the doctor's dooryard. Marianne gave Bonnie a bright smile and even Angela didn't seem upset by it all. Archie and Slinky were chattering with a few other boys, and even Slinky's mischievous laugh drifting over to the girls wasn't at all irritating. They sat and waited for their inspection—just like a happy group on holiday. And Bonnie was part of this group!

What a great feeling—finally to be one of the Lang kids, thought Bonnie.

After she checked everyone, Miss Reid gave each child another information sheet for parents. The treatment would have to be continued for a week. Bonnie was thankful her parents hadn't caught the lice from her. And in one week, this horrible time would be over.

As the Lang kids trooped past the Keene school, they did not need to shout out Bonnie's poem. Classes were going on and the blinds were drawn on the street side of the schoolhouse. Archie saw one student sharpening his pencil and peering out from behind the green window shade. But that was the only sign of life.

All the three-mile walk home, Bonnie was very popular. Slinky wanted to walk beside her, but Archie kept giving him angry looks and nudged him away. Secretly, Bonnie was happy now about the lice. As terrible as they were, the infestation had brought everyone together. And Bonnie finally felt as though she belonged.

When the tired, coal-oiled children finally sank into their seats in their little schoolhouse, Mr. McDougall stood up to speak. "Now you are going to be busy—*ahem*—bees for the rest of the day," he said. "You will notice I said bees, not fleas." Mr. McDougall laughed at his own joke but again, none of his pupils smiled. Even the senior boys did not like his humour anymore.

Mr. McDougall continued with a scowl, "This afternoon, you are all going to clean this school from top to bottom. You are going to fire up that stove and heat water. Then you'll put this Lysol in the water and wash the place from stem to stern—every inch!"

Mouths opened in amazement. Slinky stood up slowly and cleared his throat.

"Well?" said Mr. McDougall. "If you have anything worth saying, then spit it out, boy."

"I, for one, do not intend to scrub this school today," Slinky shot back. "We have walked all the way to Keene and back two days in a row. And we still have lice treatments ahead of us! We ain't gonna clean the schoolhouse. If you're not going to do any teaching, I'm going home."

Mr. McDougall's face turned bright red. He looked as though he would soon explode. He took up the strap on his desk and fingered it menacingly.

Then Slinky turned to his classmates. "Mr. McDougall is paid to keep the school clean. If he asks me nicely another day, I might help, but I ain't gonna be told to do it today. Follow me, kids!" The boy's lanky body headed toward the door and

186

disappeared into the vestibule. The sound of his footsteps blended with the creaking of the rickety steps.

Mr. McDougall stared down the aisle and out the open door in surprise.

Then they could all hear Slinky starting to chant Bonnie's poem:

"Beware of our Cooties,
Fear our disease,
We'll sting you like hornets,
We'll..."

Suddenly, Bonnie could not stay sitting there any longer. Slinky was right. She jumped up and marched down the aisle to the door. Outside, she ran to join Slinky.

Everyone—all the pupils and the teacher—stared in shock.

Then, in one wave, all the Grade Seven and Eights marched out the door, leaving their books behind. In a jumbled mob, all the others followed. Once outside, they rushed across the long front yard.

Archie shouted, "Wait for us!"

Slinky and Bonnie turned around. As they all came together in a group, the whole school started to sing.

"Beware of our Cooties,
Fear our disease,
We'll sting you like hornets,
We'll bite you like fleas,
And if you don't want to die,
Then you'd better just freeze!"

Then the Lang school kids shouted at the top of their lungs,

"FREEZE! FREEZE! FREEZE!"

As they wound through the village, the pupils sang the chorus over and over again.

Beside the bridge at the far end of town, the children from the village said goodbye to the farm kids—Bonnie and the Johnsons. And Slinky shouted, "Three cheers for our poet, Bonnie!"

"Hip, hip, hooray!" yelled the crowd.

Along with the Johnsons, Bonnie waved goodbye before she turned off the dirt road that snaked alongside the Indian River. The sun shone warmly down on Bonnie's bright smile as she skipped home.

NINETEEN: CONSEQUENCES

"Anti-I-Over!" The shouts of the Lang schoolchildren rang out. It was just after four o'clock on the Thursday following the Cootie Kids' trek to Keene and the Big Walkout. They had all gone to school wondering what would happen to them but nothing did. Mr. McDougall did not even mention the incident. All day, the expected thunderbolt did not hit. Bonnie felt sure he was just delaying the inevitable to make them suffer more. But at the end of the day when nothing had happened, she started to think that maybe Slinky was right.

"He probably realizes he's wrong and won't mention it again," Slinky had said. But Bonnie was not so sure. Something must have happened to make him change his mind. She was sure they would find out about it sometime. But better later than sooner, she decided.

Now, Bonnie was glad they were playing Anti-I-Over instead of baseball. She was seldom to blame for putting her side out—unlike baseball. She was a fairly good runner. So when the person with the ball came running round and told everyone to freeze, Bonnie was always far from the fence. Also, she was able to throw the rubber ball over the roof and no one, not even Bonnie, could predict where it would land on the other side. An advantage in this game.

"Anti-I-Over!" shouted Archie as he threw the ball to the top of the roof. It didn't quite make it and slid back down. He probably did that on purpose, Bonnie thought, for Archie had a strong swing with the ball. But sometimes this approach put the other side off guard.

Archie aimed again and this time a strong gust of wind from the northwest blew the ball right back to them.

As the group watched the ball's descent yet again, Bonnie saw a huge black cloud rolling in behind and above the roof. In fact, a big shadow seemed to have encompassed the whole roof and both sides. A dampness filled the air.

"We'll be drenched soon," shouted someone from the shed's other side.

Then they came running around from the back and up and over the fence. Half a dozen pupils including Bonnie grabbed their bookbags off the school stoop and loped across the yard. The clouds had come up suddenly and might pass over. But maybe not.

"Bye," some yelled to others. But Bonnie, Archie, and Angela just ran together toward the big gate and the winding Indian River Road toward their homes.

Then Bonnie lapsed into walking and back to running again till she came to the cow field. She started rounding up the cows. Dad would not mind her bringing them home early if it was going to rain. They wouldn't eat much in the rain anyway.

"Sic 'em, Boots," she yelled, even though the dog was nowhere in sight. That started them off. Bonnie had to chase only one cow lingering under the big maple tree—the worst place to be in a thunderstorm.

She puffed and panted as she took the cows up the side

hill. It was shorter this way but steep. She'd be glad when she got them to the fenced lane where she could go a little more slowly and she could keep them all confined to a single or double line. Running all over the field was not an easy way to bring in the herd—especially on these sharp but short hills. She wished that Boots had met her. She could only fool the cows for a little while before they caught on that Boots was not there to nip at their heels.

Bonnie and the cows were coming down the hill in the long lane before Boots spotted them and came running. In no time, she and Boots got the cows in the barnyard.

"Whew!" she grumbled, as she closed the gate. "I'm glad that's over." Cows always got restless before a storm. So now she relaxed and sauntered toward the house. If it poured, she could easily make it to shelter. Actually, the sky did not look any more ominous than it had in the schoolyard when they'd broken up their game.

Bonnie stepped through the back door. Mum shouted down the stairs. "Get at your chores, Bonnie! Hurry and feed the young chickens. Then pick up the mail."

Boots came dashing up just as Bonnie started out across the field toward the chicken coop with a full pail of water. "Back, Boots," she said a little sternly. Bonnie had grown to love him almost as much as she'd loved her cat, Shadow, but she didn't want to spill a drop of this water intended to fill the water jugs.

"It's okay, Boots," she said soothingly. He wagged his tail and walked beside her at a safe distance from the water pail.

He was now very skilled at herding the cows, and Bonnie always took him as a bodyguard when she went to pick up the mail. It was the pigs she was afraid of. They pastured in the grassy field in front of the house. And one pig was growing very big. He was no longer friendly like the smaller ones.

As Bonnie walked across the field, the sky grew almost black. Even though the storm had been threatening for some time, now it was promising to be a riptailsnorter—as Dad would say. She could see her dad lightly tapping the reins on the horses' backs in the hillside field to the west, by the main gravel road. He wanted to finish seeding before the rain hit.

Bonnie pulled open the door to the chicken coop and rushed inside. She picked up the turned-over sealers that Mum had set up as watering jugs. She threw the bit of stale water out the door, rinsed each jug, and then filled it with fresh water. The water eased out slowly for the chicks now crowding around. Then she set down the empty pail and went over to the big barrel of feed in the corner. She dipped out full scoops and poured them one by one into the big wooden feeder in the centre of the floor. The plump chickens fluttered around the fresh grain seed. There would be plenty to last till the next night.

Bonnie hurried outside. She lifted the makeshift hook on the door over the nail in the doorframe. Then she ran across the field. Already she could feel a few sprinkles of rain. But maybe that wouldn't be so bad. The rain might just drown out a few of those horrible lice and ease up the smarting sores caused by the coal oil.

At the road, Bonnie flipped up the front flap of the tin mailbox. In it was a single letter—addressed just to her. It was from Grandma Brown. She'd recognize that smooth, flowing scrawl anywhere. Delighted, she tore it open.

My dear grandchild,

It was nice to hear that Angela and Archie have been such good friends to you, and I am glad that you are now happy. I am so lonesome to see you but we cannot likely visit this summer as we had hoped. The grain seeding is taking longer than expected because of the rainy weather we've been having here in Massassaga, but the pea crop may be ready to harvest early...

Tears blurred Bonnie's eyes as she read. Then big blobs of rain dropped on the page, so she stuffed the letter in her pocket—the rest of it unread—and started to run.

She was puffing as she ran across the field. The wind was picking up now. Bonnie raced ahead the few hundred feet to the chicken coop—and stopped dead. The door was flapping!

Just then the larger pig roared out of the chicken coop and headed straight for Bonnie. She screamed, and Boots came from nowhere. Barking loudly, he stood in front of her. The pig turned away and Boots chased him all the way to the barn.

Bonnie reached up and touched the door hook. Maybe she had not latched the door carefully enough. The pig must have nosed it open. She stared through the doorway. The chickens were no longer pecking away at their feed. Instead, they were all crowded in one corner, heaped up on top of one another— limp and lifeless. There was no sound and no movement from the corner. All she could see was a big, soft, bulging pile of feathers high against the wall—no sign of heads or feet—only spread-out wings.

Bonnie stepped inside. She stood very still and stared in horror past the over-turned trough and the sealers at the pile of chickens. There was no sign of any blood or abuse: That rampaging pig must have scared them so much that they had crowded together and suffocated.

Then, blinded by tears, she staggered out the door. But this time, she put the hook over the nail very carefully. Then she tried to open it. The door held.

Bonnie walked slowly in a daze toward the house. The reality of what had happened swept over her like a great cloud. One thing was certain. Her parents were depending on those chickens. They would have provided eggs for baking, and, later, the occasional meal of chicken and dumplings. Most of the eggs would be sold so Mum would have money to buy other groceries and all the little things she missed having. Now the chickens were dead.

There would be no hens this year. Mum would be too proud to tell anyone, so there would be no replacement hens from neighbours. Mum would rather let the family starve than have her neighbours feel sorry for her.

Huge drops of rain were falling steadily. Bonnie trudged slowly toward the house. Her heart was beating so loudly, she could hear it in her ears.

She knew she was in for it. She knew it was probably her fault. She must have been in such a hurry to get the mail that she hadn't put the hook over the nail. No—she *had* put the hook over the nail, she was sure of it. But had she hooked it properly? How many ways were there to put a hook over top of a nail?

Supper, dishes, the nightly coal oil treatment—all passed in a haze, as Bonnie wrestled with her conscience and her memory. She had hooked the door—it was Dad's fault the hook was so flimsy—that pig should be penned more securely— the storm was to blame—she had to tell her parents.

"I think I better check on the chicken coop," Dad said after the storm had passed. He lit the lantern and went out the door. Bonnie sat firmly holding both arms around herself.

It seemed forever before Dad returned.

"Well?" asked Mum.

"It's still raining, so I just looked out from the verandah. The chicken coop seems to be standing fine. And the door is closed."

"I'm proud of you, Thomas," said Mum. "Bet you didn't know you were such a good carpenter. And certainly, there's no need for you to walk out there in this rain."

Bonnie knew she should tell her parents, but she just could not.

"Are you all right, Bonnie?" her mother asked, when they had gone upstairs. She set the lamp down on the nightstand.

Bonnie stared up at her, unable to speak.

"The treatments will stop soon, and you'll be able to sleep without this dreadful smell. You've been very patient and brave."

After she was gone, Bonnie stared up at the ceiling for what seemed like hours, her chest tight with guilt and anxiety. When she finally fell asleep, dark dreams kept jolting her awake again.

The next morning, she was as exhausted as if she hadn't slept at all. Dully, she dressed and went down for breakfast.

* * * *

School had been a relief, but the day was over all too fast. Exhausted from her poor night's sleep, Bonnie bent low as she ran over to the cedar hedge and then turned into the dirt road that led home. The sun was shining brightly, and as she walked along briskly through the woods, Bonnie couldn't believe she'd ever been scared in here. As she walked down the lane toward the barnyard, two robins were singing on the fence, and her dog jumped up to greet her. She patted the star on his forehead and said, "Down, Boots!"

She stepped into the back shed, took off her muddy rubbers and shoes, and opened the door to the dining room. As she stepped inside, she stopped in shock.

Her mother was staring right at her. Anger blazed from her eyes. The chickens!

Bonnie turned to run but hesitated. In that second, Mum caught Bonnie's arm and yanked her inside. She plunked her down on the chair just inside the door and stood staring at her daughter. There was a long silence.

Then Mum gasped out, "Our chickens are all dead! Our money—our only house money! There'll be nothing but fish again all winter—no sugar for canning—no material for clothes or even curtains—nothing for the house—nothing—nothing...!" Between each statement of loss, Mum's fists clenched at her sides as though she were keeping herself from grabbing Bonnie again.

Bonnie stared at her mother in stricken silence.

"Your dad found them this morning. The food trough was empty and knocked over against the wall. It would take a strong animal to do that! And one of the watering sealers was broken—with glass trampled on the floor. More than chickens had been in there. The pig must have gotten in, but the door was closed just fine. No pig could open that door and no pig could close it! What happened?"

"But it was the pig!" Bonnie sobbed. "The pig did it!"

"Who let the pig in?"

"I didn't let him in! It was the storm—the wind blew the hook off the nail."

"And who put him out? Who latched the coop afterward?"

Again, a silence fell heavy between them.

"That hook held through the worst of the storm in the early evening. It was closed when your dad looked out. It was still closed this morning. If only you had told us! Chickens are known for crowding when they are frightened. They should have been pulled apart as fast as possible! We might have revived some of them. Now they're *all* dead—suffocated. Why didn't you tell us?"

Winded, Mum fell into a chair. Her hair hung across her face. Her eyes were bloodshot and clouded over with despair.

Bonnie sat on the chair where her mother had left her, and buried her head in her lap, and sobbed.

Then she heard heavy footsteps coming through the back shed kitchen. The door flew open.

"Where is she?" shouted Dad.

Mum did not make a sound but she must have motioned to Dad. Bonnie heard his heavy footsteps and then she felt him grabbing her by the shoulder.

"Look at me, girl," he growled. "How did it happen?"

Bonnie raised her head and stammered out, "I...I...I'm not sure."

"Not sure! That's no answer," said Dad in a louder voice.

"The storm...it was the wind. It blew the door open. The pig got in but then he came out. I don't think he touched the chickens. But they were all crowded together when..."

"Oh, Thomas, what...are...we going to do?" Mum sobbed out.

As if in a daze, Bonnie heard her parents' voices.

"I don't know, Amy," said Dad. His voice was heavy and tired. "I don't know. I've tried my best. Every cent we have from the pigs and our cream has to pay the rent this fall and part of our debt. We can't touch it. We'll have to manage."

"You always say that. Years go by and you keep saying that, and it never gets any better. I'm only twenty-eight, and I feel seventy. I just can't take it anymore!"

"I'm doing my best!" shouted Dad. Then Bonnie heard the back door slam, and her father's footsteps faded outside. Now the only sound she could hear was her mother's sobs.

With the flock of chickens, things had been starting to look up. But now all hope was gone.

And she was to blame. She had promised herself that she would never be like her parents and have a debt. But now it had happened. She must pay them back for all the chickens she'd killed through her neglect. But how? There weren't nearly enough jobs for the grownups—let alone children! How could she ever repay her debt?

Then her mother's sobbing stopped and all was silent.

Bonnie crept quietly across the dining room. She mounted the stairs slowly, gripping the banister for support. Her head was pounding. Inside her spring bedroom, she sat down on the side of her bed and then lay out and sank into the feather mattress.

Why didn't I tell my parents about the chicken coop last night? Bonnie had known they would find out. But she had been so afraid. She had thought she could escape the blame by not telling them about what the pig had done.

She had been wrong.

She would be more careful and cheerful in all her tasks from now on. She would keep the woodbox full. She would fetch the cows on time every morning and night, and never forget to water the new little trees all along their white picket fence. She'd not keep forgetting till she saw the trees drooping in the sun.

She'd even help Mum weed the garden. Maybe Mum would let her cut the lawn with that old rusty lawnmower. And in the house, she'd be more careful when she washed and dried the dishes. If she really kept her mind on her work, she might never break another dish.

Maybe, too, if she tried even harder, she might learn to mend worn-out clothes. But the last resolve was probably one she couldn't keep. As Mum said, she did have two left hands. Some things were just too much for her. She knew that. Mum had told Bonnie many times that she couldn't sew a stitch correctly. Someday, though, she'd be a teacher and then she wouldn't need to sew anyway. That was a long way ahead. First, she would pay for the chickens. But how?

Maybe they could start another flock before fall. This time, Bonnie would take care of them. She'd be so careful. And maybe when she told Angela and Marianne and Archie, they'd insist on giving her some hens' eggs.

If only Bonnie could figure out a way to get Mum to accept them.

TWENTY: A SPOT OF SUNSHINE

Bonnie was glad to be at school, away from home, though she could hardly concentrate. Mum and Dad had listened to her apologies and her plans at breakfast in silence. Mum had said only, "Well, Bonnie, we'll see." But she hadn't sounded very hopeful.

All the pupils were still wearing old clothes because of the coal-oil cleanup. Just before lunch, Mr. McDougall kept them in their seats. "I have an announcement to make," he said.

Now, here it comes! thought Bonnie. At long last, their punishment for the walkout.

Mr. McDougall said, "The school board has hired a new teacher for the upcoming school year. She will be arriving after lunch today to see the school and to meet you."

The classroom was silent as the pupils digested this news.

"And you, sir?" asked Tom. "Will you be teaching next year?"

Mr. McDougall didn't bother to remind Tom to raise his hand. "Of course I will be teaching. I have been hired to teach Grade Eight in a Peterborough school."

A gasp travelled around the room. Everyone knew about big schools, where a teacher had only one grade in each room. They also knew that Grade Eight teachers always became principals after a while. So this explained Mr. McDougall's not bothering to punish them. Bonnie sighed in relief.

"Miss Clarke has just completed her training at Normal

School in Peterborough. She will be with us most of next week also. She will be interviewing each of you about your work to date and may even teach a few lessons."

Slinky raised his hand but Mr. McDougall ignored him. "I expect you all to give her your complete attention. Be respectful or you will answer to me." Everyone knew that a few young teachers in that school had had a difficult time disciplining students. Mr. McDougall wanted to nip any problems in the bud.

* * * *

Streaks of afternoon sunlight streamed across the clean, fresh classroom when Miss Clarke arrived. She was wearing a blue cotton dress with a wide collar and a slight flare to the skirt. All eyes were on her as Miss Clarke stepped sedately to the front. She placed her small schoolbag on the desk, then turned to face the class.

A golden crown of hair framed her full, rosy-cheeked face, and she glowed with a sunshine of her own. She was not smiling, but her keen blue eyes twinkled. She looked up and down each row, as if she were fastening their faces in her mind forever. She appeared to like what she saw. The students, even Slinky, eagerly sat up straighter under her steady gaze.

"Greetings, everyone. I'm so pleased to be here this afternoon. I don't know all your names yet but hope to change that very soon. I would like to meet you one at a time, so I will be calling you individually for a little chat, starting right now with Grade One…Lucy Almay, please." The small girl toddled out of her seat and up to the front. Miss Clarke had pulled an empty chair beside her own and motioned the small child toward it.

"The rest of you, return to your work," Mr. McDougall barked, but Bonnie couldn't help peeking up from her book. Miss Clarke looked like an angel compared to Mr. McDougall. She could hardly wait for her turn with the new teacher.

As soon as Miss Clarke called out her name, Bonnie was on her feet and hurrying up the aisle. But then she slowed her pace. Now that it actually was her turn, she felt strangely shy. She wanted to make a good impression. She stood beside the desk, twisting her handkerchief into a knotted roll in her hands and waiting for Miss Clarke to look up from the report she was reading. No doubt it included Mr. McDougall's comments about her—maybe even the beginning of the final report card.

Then Miss Clarke motioned Bonnie to sit in the chair beside hers. Mr. McDougall always made the pupils sit on the opposite side of his desk. But this was more comfortable.

Miss Clarke glanced at the report. "I see you transferred here from the school in Massassaga at the beginning of October," she said.

"Yes."

"Where is that exactly?"

"It's in Prince Edward County—across the Bay Bridge—about four miles from Belleville."

"Did you like it there?"

"Very much." Bonnie was starting to glow with the memory.

"You've been working hard in this school, too, I see. Mr. McDougall says that you have worked ahead in all your sums and in your reading too. He says that you even listen in on lessons for the older grades."

Bonnie was not sure if this was a criticism or not. "Well, when I get my work finished, there's nothing else to do," she said. "I like listening to the other lessons. But I don't interrupt. I don't offer to answer. I really don't…" She was looking at her lap now and her voice was lowered to a whisper.

"Well," said Miss Clarke. "Why shouldn't you listen in on the other lessons? It's a good way to learn the work ahead. Bonnie, I predict that you'll be taking two years in one—and soon."

Bonnie looked up in rapture. "Do you mean it? Do you really mean it?"

"I can't make any promises until I see more of your work. But I do mean it. Pupils who can work ahead should be promoted ahead. Perhaps you would like to take home the Grade Five arithmetic textbook and reader for the summer. Would you have time to work in them at all?"

"Oh, yes. I'd make time," Bonnie promised.

"Many teachers think that pupils can get into bad habits while working on their own. If they start on the wrong track, there is no one to correct them." Miss Clarke smiled. "But I think pupils can do anything, if they have the right tools. In arithmetic, the answers are in the back of the book. I trust you'll use them only to check the accuracy of your own work.

For the reader, you will need the help of a dictionary. Do you have one at home?"

"Yes, but it's very thin. There aren't many words in it."

"Well, do the best you can. Perhaps I can find a dictionary to put in with the other books. Anyway, I'll be here the last day of June even though school is out, and if I haven't already found one for you, I will then. Just drop by sometime in the morning."

"Golly, Miss Clarke, I'll be here. Thanks."

Miss Clarke smiled and said, "You may take your seat now, Bonnie."

"Oh, thank you, Miss Anderson," Bonnie said in her excitement.

"Clarke. My name's Miss Clarke."

"Sorry, Miss Clarke," said Bonnie. She then floated to her seat in a daze of happiness. She'd finish Grades Five and Six next year—she was sure of it!

* * * *

After school, Bonnie was plodding along home. She'd been so wrapped up in meeting the new teacher that she'd forgotten about everything at home. But as soon as she'd stepped out the door, it had all come rushing back to her.

"What do you think of the new teacher?" Archie asked. His sisters had taken the shortcut across the Hubbs' farm but he had decided to go by the long route.

"She's wonderful," mumbled Bonnie.

"So why don't you sound so wonderful?" Archie asked.

"Oh, Archie! It's just terrible!" Bonnie gulped back her tears with a choking sob. "I killed the chickens!"

"Whaaat?"

"Well, it's almost the same thing. I guess I didn't fasten the chicken-coop door tight enough. And anyway, the pig got inside and scared the chickens and they were all piled up in a heap, crowded in the corner, and when I didn't tell Mum and Dad, they found them the next morning all suffocated, and now we don't have any money to buy more eggs to hatch and we won't have any all year," she finished breathlessly.

"That *is* bad," said Archie. "If only you'd told your Mum, she might have revived some of them. You could have even phoned me and I'd have come over to see what I could do."

"No! It was during that terrible storm. You couldn't have come."

"You're right. The Danfords' chicken coop fell over and their chicks were lost, too. Now folks are giving them a "bee" to build a new henhouse. The women are going to take eggs to start them up again. I'll tell my folks and the neighbours will do the same for you."

"No! My mother would never stand for it—she's too proud. The Danfords are still grieving over Grace, so the neighbours are being extra kind. And anyway, everyone's busy making their own repairs after that storm. Dad's coop stood up fine. It was really *my* fault!"

"But the storm made it worse and—"

"No, Archie. Mum truly won't take anything from anybody.

She says we have to earn our own way. I don't know what to do."

Archie turned to go up the sharp hillside road. "Don't worry, Bonnie. I'll think of something. I promise!"

Bonnie gave Archie a wan smile as she waved goodbye.

TWENTY-ONE: THE SOMETHING PROMISE

A few days later, Bonnie's father needed to have grain ground at the Lang mill, and Bonnie went along, taking her swimsuit just in case. By mid-June, the water was generally warm enough for a nice swim. And sure enough, Angela, Archie, and Marianne were already there. "You'll have lots of time for a swim," said Dad. "Several wagons are lined up ahead of me."

The sun shone brightly across the meadow on the west side of the dam, a few hundred feet from the mill. A big maple tree shaded two picnic tables between the mill and the Lang houses, farther west. People from Keene were going to have a picnic!

Angela, Archie, Marianne, and Bonnie watched from the east side of the river. "I just hope the Keene kids stay on *that* side," grumbled Marianne.

Bonnie had butterflies in her stomach as she took one step onto the log bridge and looked down. On the left, clear water gushed over the dam and foamed where it hit the stones below. On her right, the water was dark and deep—no bottom in sight. She looked along the sturdy log bridge ahead. It had a double purpose for her, for one could easily cling to the side in the deep water. She'd keep coming back and cling to those logs for a rest. Having surveyed the spot, she stepped back onto the grassy side near her friends.

"How did you finally persuade your mum and dad to let you swim here where the river is so deep?" asked Archie. "I thought we'd have to go and help you do it."

"Her mum knows we'll look out for Bonnie," said Angela. A whistling sound came from behind them and everyone turned around.

Slinky and Tom were coming along the grassy path. Their full brown wool bathing suits slouched a little from narrow shoulder straps.

"Look!" said Bonnie, pointing at the new arrivals. "No towels or dry clothes!"

"They just run around in their bathing suits all day. Keeps them cool," sighed Archie, looking back over his shoulder. "I can't say I blame them." Archie was scratching a freckled shoulder, now peeling from a burn.

"No one seems to keep track of them much," said Angela. She stepped onto the bridge with Marianne and Bonnie following. "I'm not waiting for them. Let's go."

"Look over there at all those Keene kids," said Bonnie.

"Most Saturday afternoons, some group has a picnic there," said Angela. "Looks like their parents are here, too."

"The boys are coming onto the bridge. Why don't they just swim over there?" asked Bonnie.

"I hope they don't think they're going to swim with us," said Marianne. "Look at those awful bathing suits!"

"They've got no tops!" exclaimed Bonnie. She thought all bathing suits had tops. It was a little shocking to see them without.

The Keene boys were coming closer now. Angela and Bonnie backed off the bridge and onto the grass again. But

Marianne stood still in the middle of the narrow bridge and eyed the boys warily.

"Well if it isn't the three Misses—Louse, Critter, and Cootie—coming for a swim!" shouted a loud boy with sandy hair flopping over his freckled nose. He wore a blue, silky bathing suit with a shirred waist. His chest was bare. Two others, with their dark brown hair lifting slightly in the breeze, were dressed the same.

"Go back and swim in Rice Lake," yelled Archie, pushing past his sister to stand beside Marianne. Slinky and then Tom pounded past Bonnie and Angela and halted right behind Archie and Marianne.

"This here is our swimming hole," said Slinky, his arms folded. He sauntered out in front of the Lang kids. "If you want us to share it, you better keep a civil tongue in your head! And go back to the other side of the river!"

"Bug Town doesn't own the river!" yelled one of the Keene boys. "Cootie Kids from Bug Town don't own no river!"

In one leap, Slinky bounded ahead and pushed the loud-mouthed boy. But Slinky tottered and lost his balance. Into the deep river he shot with a mighty splash.

Tom came next and threw a punch at the other boy, who dodged. Tom went flying into the deep water.

Bonnie gasped.

"Don't worry," said Angela. "They can all swim like fish. But they shouldn't fight in the water. *That* can be dangerous."

"Yeah," said Archie. "Look!" Two of them had jumped in after Slinky and were holding him underwater.

Archie dove for the spot and pulled at the nearest boy who held Slinky.

"Help! Help! Help!" screamed Angela. "They're drowning Slinky!"

Tom was now helping Archie, but the three Keene boys still had Slinky. They pulled him up once for air as he sputtered like a fountain, then pushed him under again.

"Let him go, Henry!" yelled two Keene men from across the river. One man came running along the log bridge and dove right in—clothes and all. The boys let Slinky go. He'd gone limp. The man grabbed him and held his head above water while Archie and Tom swam alongside. Then they helped to push Slinky up to the other Keene man, who laid Slinky on his stomach on the bridge.

Slinky coughed and choked and sputtered up water. At last, he sat up, looking pale, his eyes and nose running.

"That was scary," Bonnie said.

"He'll be fine. He can hold his breath a long time," said Archie. "And it's a good thing. I'd have been a goner."

The nasty boys had all swum to their own side and were surrounded by women who were shouting angrily at them. One had a huge, wooden, ladling spoon, and she used it to hit one boy across the back. It was probably her own son, Bonnie thought. It was almost funny.

"Sorry," said a Keene man. "The swimming spot is all yours—we won't let any of them back in today."

Bonnie just shuddered. She didn't even want to go swimming now.

"That'll be their punishment," the man added. "They'll get plenty of ribbing from the others, too. And they'll just have to take it!"

Bonnie didn't think that was enough punishment.

Tom, Archie, and Marianne had already jumped off the log bridge and into the water. Marianne held her nose as she hit the deep, dark water with a mighty splash.

Slinky blew his nose with his left hand and wiped water out of his eyes with the back of his other hand. He sat there, still on the log bridge, and let his feet dangle in the water.

"C'mon in, Bonnie," said Marianne. "The water's great. It's so much easier to swim in deep water. It just holds you up. C'mon, Angela."

Angela smiled, stood up, and clasped her hands over her head. She cut the water with a perfect smooth dive. It was just like Angela to do everything perfectly. Was there anything she couldn't do? Bonnie wondered.

Bonnie sat down next to Slinky. They were alone on the bridge now. "Are you all right, Slinky?" she asked softly.

"Sure," he choked out in a hoarse voice.

Across the river, the adults were packing up their dishes and collecting their noisy children. Bonnie looked over anxiously.

"They won't come back now," said Slinky. "Not after their parents took them over there. Why don't you go for a swim?"

Bonnie hesitated and then mumbled, "I like to swim where I can touch the bottom."

"Don't worry," said Slinky. "I'll get you if you need help."

"But don't you need to rest some more?"

212

"No. I'll come back for you," said Slinky. Then he stood and dove into the river. Children on both sides of the river watched as he swam, his arms cutting the water with smooth strokes. He silently sped up the river. He was showing off again. But Bonnie didn't mind at all when he swam swiftly back and held out his hand to her.

Gingerly, she slid off the log bridge and into the water. Angela had been right. It was easier swimming in deep water. Slinky kept right beside her, even when she turned around and headed for the bridge again.

Then he crawled up on the bridge and held out his hand. Smiling up at him, Bonnie took it and then shivering, she grabbed her towel from the bridge.

Archie suddenly rose from under the water and crawled up beside Bonnie and Slinky.

"I've got news for you, Bonnie," he said. "Marianne says her dad's organizing a farewell for Mr. McDougall in the town hall. They'll be introducing the new teacher also. There'll be a real concert—with songs and recitations. The biggest event of all will be a spelling bee. And there'll be kids competing from the schools around."

Bonnie turned to stare at Archie. "Really! Oh Archie! Are you sure? That's grand! About the spelling bee, I mean." She could hardly believe such an event would be happening. Then she grabbed her towel and, throwing it around herself, she said, "But maybe it's just for the older kids, Archie."

"Actually, there'll be a Junior *and* a Senior spelling bee."

"You'll win, Bonnie," said Slinky. "We'll show those Keene

kids. I bet you could even beat the Peterborough kids!"

"It's just the country schools," said Archie. "But Keene will be one of them. They always accept a challenge."

"I'll think about it," said Bonnie, as casually as she could. As she looked over to the road she saw Dad driving his team and wagon across the bridge from the mill. He had a fresh load of chop. "I better go," she said. "Bye, Archie. Bye, Slinky."

Bonnie ran off the bridge and bent to snatch her bag of clothes from the grass. Archie followed her. "Bonnie, wait! There's more. I haven't told you the best part yet. There'll be a cash prize!"

Bonnie spun around. *A cash prize?*

"How much?" she asked breathlessly.

"I'm not sure. But I'd say at least twenty-five cents. Maybe more," Archie replied.

"Small eggs are five cents a dozen. That could buy sixty small eggs or half that many big eggs!"

"You got it!"

Bonnie grinned widely at Archie and raced over to where her father was waiting.

Clambering up onto the wagon seat, she plunked down beside Dad. A spelling bee! That was right up her alley! Of course, she'd get picked for the Junior competition! Mr. McDougall didn't like her much, but he'd want his school to win. What luck! Maybe she'd be able to win some money yet. It wouldn't be enough, but it would be a start!

"Cat got your tongue?" Dad asked.

Bonnie laughed.

214

"No, Dad. I was just thinking about a spelling bee." Then she told Dad all about it, but she didn't mention the cash prize. She'd keep that hope to herself for now.

TWENTY-TWO: THE SPELLING BEE

The evening of June 29, 1937, was clear and bright. A breeze blew fresh and light through the auditorium in the old town hall as Bonnie and her mother stepped in through a side door. Dad was still tying Duke up in the shed, but when he arrived, he would be surprised. The place was packed with folks from Keene, Lang, and surrounding areas. The community concert had already begun, so Bonnie and her mother stood at the door, looking for a place to sit. Mum held her new blue crocheted purse proudly under her arm while Bonnie smoothed down the front of her white cotton middy.

Just then, Slinky jumped up from his seat near the front and joined Bonnie. "Our school has the front two rows," he said. "Just follow me."

Bonnie looked up at her mother, who nodded. "Go on. I'll wait here for Dad."

Bonnie hurried along after Slinky. He motioned her to sit in the second row. There was Archie, right by the aisle, and Angela and Marianne were next. Marianne squeezed over to make a place on the bench. Bonnie stepped along in front of Archie to sit next to Marianne, and then there was another wholesale slide down the row as Slinky plunked himself down next to Archie.

"Whatever kept you?" Marianne whispered. "The Junior Spelling Bee comes right near the first. I was in a dither thinking you wouldn't make it in time."

216

Bonnie just shook her head and rolled her eyes up to the ceiling. She and Mum had tried hard to finish all the chores before Dad came in from the field, but there was still milking left to do. And it took them longer than most to get to the town hall because they'd come in the horse and buggy. There was no money to get the car going this spring.

As everyone had expected, Mr. McDougall had chosen Bonnie to represent the school for the Junior competition. She would be competing against Keene and three other rural schools—Rice Lake, Indian River, and Westwood.

Bonnie could feel her cheeks flushing as she waited. So much depended upon her winning the prize money. *Please, God*, she prayed silently. *Help me win.*

Marianne's sister Maribelle was belting out "Danny Boy" on the stage, accompanied by her mother on the piano. Both were dressed in purple chiffon with ruffles. But Bonnie wasn't really listening or watching. She kept shifting in her seat and twisting the clean, white handkerchief her mother had stuffed into the pocket of her skirt. "You'll do just fine, Bonnie. I know you will," Marianne said, to calm her down.

Now the audience was clapping loudly as Maribelle curtsied. She didn't look one bit nervous. Bonnie cleared her throat and waited.

Mr. Hubbs, smiling widely, stepped up to the lectern at the front of the stage. As master of ceremonies, he squinted at his list and opened his mouth to announce the next event. But the audience was still clapping and shouting, "Encore!"

So Mr. Hubbs stepped aside to allow his daughter and wife

to come back up on stage. This time, Maribelle launched into "The Bonnie, Bonnie Banks of Loch Lomond." That was a fine one to pick, thought Bonnie. She imagined herself, Bonnie, running off into the night to Loch Lomond because she'd lost the spelling bee. It almost made her wish she'd never been chosen for the competition.

Bonnie clutched the edge of the bench and looked down at the floor, overwhelmed by nerves. No doubt she'd lose—right in front of her parents, her school and the whole community. Surely, she could have thought of a better way to earn some money.

Finally, Maribelle was seated and Mr. Hubbs was at the lectern again. "And now the Junior Spelling Bee. Will all the contestants please come to the stage?"

"Show them up, Bonnie!" Slinky said, a bit too loudly, as Bonnie gathered up her courage and made her way to the aisle. Bonnie flushed, hoping not too many had heard the cheer.

Mr. Hubbs continued. "We are honoured this evening to have the well-known principal, Dr. Kenner, from Peterborough Collegiate and Vocational School, to adjudicate this competition. Dr. Kenner was already at our school to pick up the entrance examinations written by our graduating class so they can be marked by teachers chosen by the Ontario Ministry of Education. We're very pleased that he's agreed to stay with us a little longer to adjudicate both the Junior and the Senior spelling bees. The Junior includes Grades Four and under; the Senior, Grades Eight and under."

Dr. Kenner, dressed in a fine brown suit and yellow plaid tie, stepped up to the stage as the audience clapped. He shook hands with Mr. Hubbs.

"It is indeed a great honour for me to be here this evening. I do see how interested your community must be in your school activities, as so many are here to participate tonight and to bid farewell to Mr. McDougall. Lang's loss will be Peterborough's gain when he continues his career in our fair city in September." Then he looked down at the little brown spellers on the lectern.

By now, two girls from the other side of the auditorium and one boy from the middle had come up on stage beside Bonnie. But Bonnie barely glanced at them. She twisted her handkerchief so hard, she felt as if it was going to rip in two. Then she looked down directly at the Lang kids in the first two rows, where Angela and Marianne were beaming proudly up at her. Even Tom and Slinky were jumpy with excitement. A surge of courage seemed to bolster Bonnie for the moment.

Next, she glanced over to where Mum and Dad were sitting. They, too, were staring up at her with expectation in their eyes. They knew she was a good speller. Maybe this would be another small victory! And even if she didn't win, maybe Mum would see that Bonnie was trying to be brave. But she didn't feel very brave.

Then she stared at Dr. Kenner, wondering which spellers he'd use. Unfortunately, they were all the same colour, so it was hard to tell. But, of course, it would be *The Canadian Speller Book One* because it covered Grades Three to Six.

Mr. Hubbs turned and smiled at the entrants, and Bonnie began to relax a little. "Let us hold all applause until the competition is over, for we must remember that these pupils have all been chosen from their schools as top spellers. We don't want to distract them from doing their best. All do deserve our applause—but at the end." Mr. Hubbs then nodded to Dr. Kenner, who began reading out the words to be spelled.

At first, they were easy. Bonnie couldn't believe that the boy and one girl went down on *cracker*—not really a difficult word at all. The judge nodded at her.

"*Cracker*. C-r-a-c-k-e-r," Bonnie said easily.

Soon, she and another girl, named Jennie, were the only ones left. They both knew that Dr. Kenner would now be reading out words higher than their grade level. Bonnie was glad. She'd taken most of the Grade Five words the previous spring. She suspected that the other girl had never seen them before.

"*Jumping*," said the adjudicator, turning to Jennie. That was a Grade Four word. It had appeared in the spelling list just last week. Bonnie sighed. Maybe she wouldn't win after all. Jennie spelled it quickly and correctly.

"*Chopping*," said Dr. Kenner, his grey-green eyes looking straight through Bonnie.

Tricky, thought Bonnie. She knew that *jumping* did not double the "p" but *chopping* did—she recognized the word from the Grade Five list she'd studied back in Massassaga. "*Chopping*," Bonnie began, then drew a big breath.

Immediately, she launched into a major coughing spell. Dr. Kenner raised both eyebrows as he waited.

Finally, Bonnie squeaked out: "*Chopping.* C-h-o-p-p-i-n-g." Where did that cough come from? Bonnie wondered in a panic. She hadn't coughed in a long time. It was that old nervous habit of hers. How horrible. But she must drop it from her thoughts. If ever she needed to think, it was now!

"Correct, Bonnie."

The words continued: *women, weighed, forgotten, addition, geography, handkerchief, success.* There were more from the Grade Five list than the Grade Four.

"And now, Jennie," said Dr. Kenner.

Would it be another Grade Five word? Bonnie wondered. She hoped so.

Dr. Kenner cleared his throat. "*February.*"

Bonnie knew that was a tricky word, since most people pronounced it "Feb-u-ary." But she was not fooled and could hardly wait for Jennie to answer.

"*Febuary.* F-e-b-u-a-r-y," said Jennie.

"I'm sorry, you are wrong—but the competition is not over. Bonnie, please spell *February.*"

"*February.* F-e-b-r-u-a-r-y," said Bonnie. That felt good, but there was still a long way to go. Everyone knew that the second one to spell a given word had an advantage, so she would be given another word to spell correctly as well. Then, if Bonnie made a mistake on that second word and Jennie spelled it the right way, the two girls would be tied for winner. But if Bonnie spelled the second word correctly, she would win the competition. Bonnie took in a deep breath as she waited. She hadn't started coughing...yet.

"Bonnie, your word is *carbohydrate*."

Bonnie smiled. She'd met this word in the Grade Five speller. "*Carbohydrate*. C-a-r-b-o-h-y-d-r-a-t-e."

"Correct!" said Dr. Kenner. "We have our winner!"

The audience erupted in applause. Archie and Slinky let out a couple of loud cheers.

As for Bonnie, she could hardly believe that this had really happened. She knew she could win but after she got up there, she'd been afraid her mind would go blank and she would ruin it all. But she hadn't! Slowly, a feeling of delight—and relief—crept over her.

When the clapping died down, Dr. Kenner spoke again. "You have all been fine participants and good spellers. Mr. Hubbs, I believe, has a ribbon for each of you."

Mr. Hubbs came forward and pinned a ribbon on each child's left shoulder. Then he gave Bonnie an envelope, which Bonnie knew had a hard coin in it. She felt it and was certain it was a twenty-five-cent piece.

The pupils stepped down to more cheers.

Mr. Hubbs spoke again. "We are now going to continue with the Senior Spelling Bee, since Dr. Kenner has kindly agreed to judge it as well. Then he will be leaving us to travel home to Peterborough. Would the Senior contestants please come up now?"

While two girls came up from the left side and one boy from the right, Mr. Hubbs stepped down from the stage and came right over to Bonnie. "This competition is for Grade Eight and under," he said. "If you wish, you may compete in this spelling bee too."

"No, sir," Bonnie shook her head. She was wanting only to go and sit down between her friends. Her knees were shaking too much to stand there any longer. Best she make it quietly to her seat. "But thank you."

"Well, you'll have a few minutes to think about it," said Mr. Hubbs. "Keene's contestant has only just arrived, so it won't start for a few minutes."

"Why not give it a try, Bonnie?" Archie whispered.

Mr. Hubbs was eyeing a boy who'd come in the side door a moment ago. The Keene teacher pointed him toward the platform. Bonnie, Archie, and Slinky all looked over at the same time. The contestant was Henry, one of the three boys who'd nearly drowned Slinky at the Mill Pond!

Archie and Slinky sat up straight, as if struck by lightning.

"He should be ruled out!" Archie hissed indignantly.

"Or struck out!" Slinky growled, turning to Bonnie and giving her a knowing look.

Bonnie stared back in disbelief. Slinky was asking her to beat that boy! She would like to. But what if she lost and he won? Wouldn't that make it worse? Then, as she stared at the ruffian, she realized she must stand up to him—for Lang School, for all her friends there now, for Archie, and for Slinky, whom he'd nearly drowned.

In that split second, she had made her decision. Bonnie got up. She didn't feel shaky anymore. Not even thinking about her cough or her twisted handkerchief this time, she took her place beside the other pupils.

Dr. Kenner announced, "This competition is for Grade Eight *and under*. So we have encouraged the winner of the first competition to join us."

As before, Dr. Kenner began with simpler words and then moved on to the more difficult ones. One girl spelled out on *rheumatism*. But Bonnie spelled it the right way. The other girl went down on *interpretation*, but Henry spelled it correctly.

So Bonnie and Henry were now left to battle it out one-on-one. Bonnie was almost a head shorter than the skinny Keene boy, but she didn't look at him or anyone as the new words came. Instead, she focused on each word in her mind's eye. The words flew back and forth: *masquerade, fascinate, collateral*. There was deep silence in the old town hall as each word was presented.

"*Scissors*," said Dr. Kenner. Bonnie wished she'd had that one. She could have spelled that as easily as rolling off a log.

"*Scissors*. S-i-s-s-o-r-s," said Henry.

Dr. Kenner shook his head. Then he turned to Bonnie.

"*Scissors*. S-c-i-s-s-o-r-s." Bonnie spelled the word correctly. But she still had to spell one more correctly.

"*Crocheting*," said Dr. Kenner.

"*Crocheting*. C-r-o-c-h-e-t-i-n-g," Bonnie said without hesitation. She may not have been good at cutting patterns with Mum's scissors or at crocheting doilies, but she knew how to spell the words! She'd seen them many times in her mother's pattern books.

224

"We have our winner—our two-time winner—Bonnie Brown from Lang School. Congratulations, Bonnie, and congratulations to all our students who have done so well."

Henry looked over at Bonnie and glowered, but Bonnie smiled at him and said quietly, "You're a really good speller. You nearly beat me out!" He smiled back, rather weakly. But still, it was a smile. Bonnie wondered if he remembered that she'd seen him bullying Slinky.

This time, Dr. Kenner proudly handed her an envelope. Then, once again, all the participants were ribboned, and the town hall was filled with applause as they walked back to their seats. Archie and Slinky were hopping up and down like jumping beans.

"Will you two stop it!" Bonnie laughed. "Everyone's looking at us!"

"And so they should! You beat out that Henry bully, and you're our heroine!" Slinky jumped up so high Bonnie was sure he'd crash-land and he almost did, but Archie broke his fall. Marianne and Angela broke out into fits of giggles and gave Bonnie a big bear hug.

Finally, the noise and the jumping and the hugging stopped, and Mr. Kenner announced, "These pupils are all, indeed, excellent spellers. The words for the Grade Eight and under contest were taken from the Grade *Nine* speller." Whoops of surprise and awe broke out around the auditorium, and there was another round of applause.

Bonnie was so excited she could hardly concentrate on the rest of the performance. There were a few funny recitations by community members and some joshing on stage about school events, and then speeches of congratulations to the departing Mr. McDougall.

Bonnie wasn't clutching the edge of the bench anymore. She was hanging on tightly to the two envelopes in her hand. The second one seemed to have a quarter in it, too. And was there a second, smaller coin in one corner of that envelope?

"It has been a pleasure," Mr. McDougall was now saying, "to teach such bright pupils and to live in such a fine community." When he went to sit down, amidst a roar of clapping, he wiped his eyes with a huge, white linen handkerchief. Bonnie was surprised. She didn't know he had any feelings at all.

"Now," said Mr. Hubbs. "We come to the last event—the door prize. I hope you've all put your names in that box by the door!" Mr. Johnson carried the box up to the edge of the platform and gave it to Mr. Hubbs. The master of ceremonies picked it up with both hands and shook it well. Then he asked the smallest girl in the first row to come up on stage to pick out a name.

Smiling, Mr. Hubbs bent over to hold the box for the little red-headed girl in the frilly, blue dress. "Now, pull out just one slip of paper."

The little girl giggled as she grabbed one piece of paper and handed it up to Mr. Hubbs.

"Lawrence Smith." He stared down at Slinky, who looked as if he'd been struck by lightning for the second time that evening. Then he came to his senses and ambled slowly up the stairs as if he couldn't care less about winning. But Bonnie could see he was all smiles.

The prize was a huge box of chocolates.

As Slinky clambered back down the steps, Mrs. Hubbs stepped over to the piano and started to play "God Save the King."

"Bonnie, I'm proud of you," said Mr. McDougall. He'd come over to congratulate Bonnie after the anthem was over. "And next school year, I'm sure you'll be able to do those two grades."

"Thank you, Mr. McDougall—and I hope you like your new school." Bonnie guessed he could be nice after all—that is, when one got to know him better.

Bonnie soon found herself at the centre of a crowd of schoolmates.

"Three cheers for Bonnie!" said Archie.

"Hear, hear!" said Slinky, his mouth full of chocolate. "You showed 'em!"

Bonnie thought back to the time the boys had swung her up into the tree in the schoolyard. She remembered her awful loneliness when she'd first moved to the farm. What a difference! Now, those days seemed like a lifetime ago.

"Bonnie, we have to go!" called Mum from the doorway, adjusting her hat.

"But…" Bonnie was about to ask to stay longer when she remembered she had something more important to do.

Bonnie waved to her friends and followed her mother, who was already slipping out the side door.

As they scurried between the cars next to the town hall

on the way to their horse and buggy, Mrs. Johnson caught up with them. "We're really proud of your wee lass, Amy. A grand performance, Bonnie!"

"Thank you, Alice," said Mum. "I must say I was surprised—"

"Sure was good to see that Henry spelled down!" Angela interrupted. Archie was standing beside her, grinning from ear to ear.

"Bonnie likes to read novels. I guess that helps her spelling," said Mum.

"Those last two words are in most *needlework books*," said Mrs. Johnson. "She's been reading them, too, I'd guess!"

"Yes, she has—just lately. Maybe she'll even learn how to follow their directions one of these days." Still, Bonnie could tell that Mum was proud of her by the way she held her back up so straight and tall.

"Of course, she will. She's a bright lass."

By the time Bonnie and her mother reached the shed, a number of cars were already gone and Dad was sitting in the buggy. Mum swung up nimbly and gave Bonnie her hand to help her get in. The grand winner of the spelling contest landed successfully, if a bit clumsily, on the seat beside her mother.

"Getty-up, Duke," said Dad, still holding the reins tightly, for he didn't want Duke racing through town at a terrible speed. Then he peered around to look at his daughter's happy face. "I'm so proud of you, Bonnie," he said. "I knew you'd be a winner in the junior competition, but I could hardly believe my eyes when you out-spelled those Grade Eights!"

"Now, Thomas, don't give her a swelled head. But, yes, Bonnie, we are very proud of you tonight. Just don't get conceited. Pride goeth before a fall, you know."

"But, Mum, I've got money now! Let's count it and then put it in your purse."

"Yes, I should keep it for you. You wouldn't want to lose it! But we can wait to count it until we get home."

"Can't we count it now?" Bonnie begged.

"Oh, Amy," said Dad. "Let Bonnie count it. How much is it?" Bonnie put the envelopes on Mum's lap and Mum opened them carefully. There lay two quarters and two dimes.

"Seventy cents!" Mum said. "That's a lot of money, Bonnie. I'm amazed!" She carefully put the coins in her little black purse and snapped it shut. Then she tucked the small purse safely into her big blue crocheted bag. "Whatever do you plan to do with all that money?"

"Well, I already have some plans—big plans," Bonnie said. "I want to use all my prize money to buy more eggs. Then we'll have lots of chickens!"

Mum gasped and looked over at Bonnie.

"Yes!" Bonnie went on. "Seventy cents will buy us seven dozen big eggs. That's eighty-four eggs. Almost as many as last winter! I do wish it were a hundred, though."

"That *will* be enough for a hundred," said Mum breathlessly, "because ten cents a dozen is what they charge folks in the store for big eggs, but farmers' wives get paid only half that and we can buy directly from a number of women I know…"

"But, Bonnie, we don't want to take your prize money. You

229

wanted a dictionary. Now's your chance to buy your very own," Dad interjected.

"I can borrow one from the school for the summer. Miss Clarke said I could go by tomorrow and pick it up."

"Well, I don't know," Mum murmured. Bonnie wasn't sure she'd ever heard her mother sound so unsteady before.

"No, this money must go for the chicks," Bonnie insisted. "Please. I want to do this—it's why I entered the spelling bee in the first place!"

"By George! That's great, Bonnie," said Dad, slapping the reins gently on Duke's back. "We'll even have eggs this winter."

"And I'm going to watch them really well this time."

"Thank you, Bonnie." Dad laughed. "You're already beginning to sound like a hen clucking over her chicks." Even Mum laughed at that. Bonnie could tell she was relieved.

"Hey, wait!…Wait!" yelled someone coming up behind the buggy.

"Did you hear someone call?" Dad asked, pulling on the reins to slow Duke down.

"Wait, wait!" the person called again, panting this time.

"What on earth?" Dad asked. "Is there something wrong?" Then he yelled, "Whoa!" and pulled on the reins to stop Duke in his tracks.

Dad and Mum looked around. Bonnie didn't need to turn her head because she knew the voice!

Slinky came rushing up to Bonnie's side of the buggy, his long, straggly hair flying behind him. He handed her a parcel.

"Top row's all gone," he gulped, "but nobody touched the

bottom layer—I saved that for you!"

"Gee, thanks, Slinky!" Bonnie managed to say, a bit shocked.

Then Slinky disappeared into the gathering darkness.

Dad winked at Mum as Bonnie opened the box with the utmost care. A soft, delicious aroma drifted up, and Bonnie stared at the chocolates, each sitting in a tiny brown paper holder. Yes, Slinky had saved the whole bottom layer for her. It was glistening there in the moonlight, just waiting to be eaten up.

But first, Bonnie held the box out to her mother. "You and Dad choose first."

Mum smiled and handed the box to Dad first, then took one herself. "Sure is good," said Dad, smacking his lips. "Thank you, Bonnie."

"Yes, thank you," said Mum.

Bonnie could hardly decide which one to choose but it didn't really matter. She knew she'd like any of them. She soon found she'd popped a cherry-filled chocolate into her mouth and then handed the box back to Dad. "Don't mind if I do," he said. "But you don't need to give us all your candy."

"I *want* to share them." Bonnie smiled, handing the box to Mum.

The family travelled on in happy silence. Before long, Duke was turning onto the road into the woods. Nearing home, the horse picked up his pace even in the semi-darkness, and the trees closed around them like an embrace. Bonnie stared at the beams of moonlight streaking across their path. She wasn't afraid of these woods anymore.

Then Mum said, "Bonnie, you were very brave this evening. I know how hard it was for you to stand up there in front of all those folks. Yet, you did. For you, that was no small victory. It was a big one!"

HISTORICAL NOTE

Lang is now the site of Lang Pioneer Village, a living museum, located ten minutes southeast of Peterborough, Ontario, and nestled along the banks of the historic Indian River. The Pioneer Village shows over twenty restored heritage buildings, including a working grist mill. Guides in authentic costume show visitors a glimpse into the daily lives of early pioneers through trade demonstrations, traditional crafts, rare farm animals, and heritage gardens. As well as re-enactments of historic times and tasks, the village has contest days with hay-loading, log-stacking, nail-driving, log-sawing, spelling bees, tongue twisters, three-legged races, and more. Every June, Lang Pioneer Village hosts many busloads of schoolchildren. Many days I am there, too, to give readings, sign books, and remember with today's children the turbulent days of my own childhood.

Not only Lang, but the whole of Canada suffered during The Great Depression of the twentieth century. Those years became commonly known as The Hungry Thirties or The Dirty Thirties. Yet, there were surpluses of many things—including food. The potatoes of Prince Edward Island were left to rot in the fields, and wheat was burned on the Prairies because no one had enough money to ship them to market. Wagonloads of tomatoes and peas from Massassaga, Ontario, were rejected by canners because those factories had no money to pay for them. In 1932, 400,000 automobiles were produced in Canadian factories but only 40,000 were sold.

There was a great deal too much of most things—apart from jobs and money.

From 1931 to 1933, thousands were laid off from their jobs with no unemployment insurance and no severance pay. Many found no new employment until the end of the decade. By 1933, Canada's unemployment rate had reached 26.6 percent, and people in every occupation were affected—from professionals to labourers. Many girls trained to be registered nurses but most could not find work until 1939, when World War II began. School teachers earned very low wages. In a number of cases, school boards, both urban and rural, could not afford to pay them, so teachers worked only for their meals and lodging. By 1936, two-thirds of Canadian young people could not find jobs because work was going to more experienced applicants. Youth actually suffered the most during this decade.

Braithwaite, Max, *The Hungry Thirties, 1930–1940*. Canada's Illustrated Heritage Series. Toronto: 1977.

ABOUT THE AUTHOR

Connie Brummel Crook has lived in the Peterborough area of Ontario, Canada, for most of her life. After attending early elementary school near Belleville, she moved with her parents to a farm near Peterborough, then to a farm north of Norwood, where she walked three miles to high school. Connie studied English, history and psychology at Queen's University before becoming a teacher. Today, Connie enjoys giving presentations at Lang Pioneer Village as part of her life-long quest to bring Canadian history to life for young people.

A young Connie Brummel with two four-legged friends. Boots, standing beside her, was her inspiration for the doggy character of the same name.